1

TAG, YOU'RE IT

Bryan Kollar

Original cover art by Rob Williams
www.Fiverr.com/cal5086

Acknowledgements and Shout Outs

Shout outs and appreciations go to the following:

- Once again, just like my previous five books, I must thank each and every person who let me use their real first and last names. To this day, I still absolutely refuse to use anything but real first and last names of people I know.
- Not only are the names of the characters real, so are the businesses! Thank you to four businesses who let me use their company name in my book:

TrackR Bravo (Page 22) – The tiny tracking device that can locate your missing or lost items using your mobile phone!

Midnight Tactical (Page 68) – My buddies gun shop! Need a gun? Give 'em a call at. 570-606-1185.

Meadow Ridge Coffee (Page 51) – A new coffee company with great awesome flavors

Cirkul (Page 46) – Flavor your ordinary water with a many different flavor to choose from. Turn the flavor wheel to make the flavor stronger or weaker!

Reolink (Page 43) – Once again, using Reolink, since my home is now protected with not one, but four of them!

Pamtri (Throughout the entire book) – This YouTube'r has some really awesome strange and demented videos on his channel. And since dreams are strange, why not use Pamtri's videos?

So here's a little surprise for my fans!

Throughout this book, there will be mention of someone's dream. That's what the book is all about – dreams!

But not only will you read about what the character dreamt about, you will get to see it, too! I went through **Pamtri's** archive and chose ones that fit. Most of the time I altered the book around the video!

So when reading the book, make sure you're around a computer or mobile device. It's not required to watch the dream to understand the book by any means, but I guarantee it's going to be fun to see the dream come to life. There will be a website given when it's time to view the dream I wrote about.

CHAPTER ONE

"How much do you think I should charge?"

"I have a better question. What person in their right mind would want to pay?"

"Oh, come on," John said, irritated at his fiancé for making fun of his invention. "Haven't you ever wished you had a video recording of your dreams?"

"Not really," Bonnie replied. "No matter how many different ways you ask that question, you're going to get the same response."

John picked up his phone and looked through the contact list. "There are at least four people here that would be willing to pay at least $100 to record their dreams."

"Is that $25 each?"

"Very funny," John said. "I can easily get $100 per recording."

"Four people, huh? Out of how many contacts? Wow, that's a whole $400. That's well worth the ten-year investment in this stupid project. Maybe you can buy me an engagement ring upgrade from the $100 model you got me three years ago. Yeah, we should give it a try after all."

That was low, John thought. *I know there will be a line at our door waiting to pay. Maybe I should rent office space. I'll call it "Dreams R Us." Nah, technically all I need is a thirty by thirty-foot room. I can easily use our guest room. There's nothing to this.*

"You'll see! When I advertise this," John said, getting defensive, "I'll bet you that within one month after going live with this, we'll have people coming back here for at least seconds and thirds, probably more. How much are you willing to lose?"

"First of all, I'm not betting you anything. And secondly, I don't want strangers in our house. You don't know the long-term effects of this thing. You're going to fry someone's brain and get sued."

"If I fry their brain, how are they going to sue me," he said jokingly. Bonnie wasn't smiling, so John eased up a bit. "Look, hun, it's not going to fry their brain. I've been using all the prototypes for the past ten years, and I'm perfectly normal. Don't you think problems would have arisen by now?"

Bonnie picked up the device and just stared at it, obviously deep in thought.

"You want to try it, don't ya? Come on. I won't even charge you."

"Nope." She wanted to try it but was afraid. The only other person John used this on suffered an incredible migraine a few seconds after it was removed from his head. In John's defense, he was informed he already had a slight headache but still wanted to give it a try. The incident was written off as just 'one of those things.' John didn't think his invention had anything to do with it, but even if it did, he's made many adjustments since then.

"I'm just thinking about how much time you wasted on that thing. The time that could have been spent together doing fun things with me." She carelessly tossed the contraption to the side.

"Hey, be careful with that!"

It was hopeless. Bonnie was dead set against the whole idea, but deep inside, John knew he'd be rich and famous someday, with or without her.

John took the DVD with his previously recorded dream and popped it into the DVD player, purposely, while Bonnie was still in the room with him. He wanted her to see the quality of the video captured from the dream he had two days ago. Before the DVD even had a chance to start, Bonnie picked up her subscription magazine from the living room coffee table. *So much for that.*

There he sat, in awe of his invention. *This is amazing!* With his head parallel to the TV, he discreetly moved his eyes in the direction of Bonnie to see if she was watching from behind her magazine, but all that remained was an empty chair. He frowned, ejected the DVD, inserted the special one without any markings, turned the TV out of view of anyone behind him and watched the footage of a sex dream he had two weeks ago. He had no idea who the female in the video was, but she certainly was a hottie, even with one breast that completely disappeared thirty seconds into the clip. If Bonnie somehow got a hold of this DVD and watched it, it was so crystal clear that she may not believe him that it was just a dream until she saw that breast disappear. Then again, if she did see this video and knew it was a dream, she'd question who this mysterious woman was and why her fiance wanted to have sex with her. *Here is the exact reason I'm going to be rich and famous. Everyone has sex dreams. Everyone would want them recorded, wouldn't they?* He sat there a bit longer, getting aroused, trying to ignore the missing breast until he heard Bonnie's voice from the other room. Startled, he shut the video off and then realized she was talking on the telephone, not directly to him.

Forget it. I'll try it on my friend, he thought. *I'm confident it's safe.*

John picked up his phone and scrolled to one of the names in his address book that he saw earlier, Yüsli Yüsöf.

"Hey, John, what's up?"

"Yüsli, my man, how's it going?"

"Ah, just chillin' with a beer, a little drunk, what can I do for ya? Want to come over and drink with me?"

"No thanks, buddy. I just put the finishing touches on my invention. I'm ready to test it on someone other than myself. You, my friend, are the chosen one! You wanna see how it works?"

"I guess your missus is still against the whole idea, ain't she."

"Unfortunately so. But that's ok, all I need is someone else to try it on. Whaddya say?"

Yüsli took a moment to respond before replying. "If this thing kills me, I'll haunt *you* in *your* dreams."

"Sweet! I'll be able to record that to a DVD, too! So I take it that's a yes?"

"Yeah, I guess so. Better do it now while I'm drunk and can't think straight. You'll have to come over here, though. I'm drunk, and I'm not driving anywhere in this cold weather. Plus, I don't know if I mentioned it yet, I'm drunk."

"Yeah, you've mentioned that a few times. Ok, I'll be right over. Leave your door unlocked so if you fall asleep before I get there, I can let myself in and just put the thing on you."

No response.

"Hello?"

No response.

"Yüsli!"

"I'm here, I'm here. Ok. I'll unlock the door now. I'm not going to last much longer, so you'll have it easy."

"Ok," John said, not sure if Yüsli is even going to make it to the door in time before passing out. "I'm leaving now. Go unlock your door, ok?"

No response.

Sigh.

CHAPTER TWO

"Hello, I'm here," John called out while he knocked on the steel door with his ring. He turned the doorknob, the door opened with ease. "Hello? Yüsli?" No response. All John heard was someone talking in the living room. It wasn't Yüsli's voice. *Damn, I don't want anyone else to know about this yet.*

"Hello? Yüsli? Anyone?"

No response.

John entered the living room to find Knight Rider, the 80's classic playing on the TV, with Yüsli passed out cold, half on the couch and half off, beer still in his hand.

Sigh.

John pried the newly opened can of beer from his hand and placed it on the table next to the nearly full KFC box. He removed the contraption from the soft custom-made padded case, placed the large ring-shaped device over Yüsli's head and flipped the joystick side switch up, then to the right, then left, then right again, and then up once more. The correct secret code lit up the entire device with blue lights, identical to Amazon's Alexa. The lights followed each other in a round chasing-type pattern, changed to yellow, and then finally green which meant it fully connected to the brain.

A huge smile came across John's face. *Of course it works, why wouldn't it?*

Within a few seconds, a second single red light came on and started flashing rapidly to show it was recording something. A blue timer also started, displaying its active recording time. Yüsli was already in a dream state. The hardest part now was the wait.

John picked up a paperback book by Sally Berneathy, "Guns, Wives and Chocolate." He was only able to read the first few sentences before the red light shut off and the timer flashed one minute ten seconds. Disappointed with the short recording time, he put the book down and went to remove the helmet when the red light came back on. It started to flash once again, and the timer continued its counting. He sat down and picked up the book again. Within a few more seconds, it stopped again, now at one minute fifteen seconds. He stared at it, waiting for it to continue. And when it didn't, he removed it from Yüsli's head, ejected the micro SD card, and inserted it into his phone. Up came Yüsli's dream.

Visit www.bryankollar.com/yusli.html
to view Yüsli's dream

*****

The dream was strange. A bit different than the dreams he had, but after all, Yüsli was a strange man. Even though the dream didn't make any sense, now he was confident his invention would work on anyone.

It seems that the KFC Yüsli had last night was somehow incorporated into the dream. John found it amusing how the Colonel held a man at gunpoint, demanding that he drive to KFC for some chicken. When KFC didn't have what the Colonel wanted, the Colonel blew up the building.

What should I call this device? Dream Video Recorder, or DVR for short… um, no, that would be too confusing. Maybe something with my last name. Anderson's Amazing… um… He gave up after just a few seconds, losing interest in thinking of a name right now, still focused on how strange this dream was. John renamed the file to the standard format he's been using for his dreams, today's date and the name of the person who had the dream. He glanced over at Yüsli, sleeping like a baby. *Is he sleeping? Did this thing kill him?* He poked Yüsli. No response. He poked him harder. Nothing. He shook Yüsli again, this time a bit too hard.

"What the hell, man! What are you doing?"

"Sorry, buddy, just making sure you're ok. How do you feel?"

No response. Yüsli was too hammered and was already fast asleep once again. John packed up his equipment and left, with all intentions of making a deal with his fiancé to give it a try. Unfortunately, if Yüsli had a migraine, he wouldn't know if it came from his invention or his inevitable hangover.

13

*****

"What's this crap? Come on, John, I thought we were gonna watch a movie."

"We are, technically. This movie was in Yüsli's head."

Bonnie was ticked off, but also quite humored. John watched Bonnie smile and try to hide a laugh.

"This makes no sense, but that Colonel is one bad-ass guy!"

John laughed and hoped the ridiculousness of the video wouldn't keep her from trying it if she did change her mind. "Dreams don't ever make sense. I bet if we tried this on you, yours would be more demented than this," said John, throwing out the hint again he wanted to try it on her.

This time she didn't say no. Her eyes shifted towards John while her head stayed in the same position, then back at the TV.

John continued. "Come on, hun, it's safe. I've been using it for years. Yüsli volunteered without a problem, what are you afraid of?"

"Yüsli was drunk. You said it yourself. Otherwise, he probably wouldn't have tried it."

"Yes, he would. He'd do anything for me, which is what you should be doing. We've been best friends forever. Look, don't you think I'd know by now if it caused problems? I've created it, I would know."

After a long moment of silence, Bonnie finally replied. "What if I get a migraine like that guy you first tried it on."

14

"Then it will go away as all migraines do. Besides, that was a one-off thing. He told me he had a headache even before we started, and I never got a headache from it, now did I?"

"Okay, but only if we can watch it together."

She had finally agreed!

"Thanks, hun."

As the hours passed, John became anxious. When Bonnie was nearly ready for bed, John was a little too eager. He brought the contraption out of its soft protective case and placed it next to her in the bathroom.

"Really, John? Come on. Give me a minute, will you? I still need to freshen up."

Feeling a little embarrassed, John just nodded and moved it from the bathroom sink to her side of the bed. Then, thinking it would still be too much, he moved it yet again to his side of the bed, and he sat on her side instead, pretending not to watch her get ready.

Bonnie watched his ridiculous antics from the bathroom mirror and knew he was incredibly anxious. She sat next to him and saw the anticipation.

"Ok. Let's get this over with, go ahead."

It was almost comical how quickly he snatched the device from his side of the bed and placed it over her head.

"Hey, this isn't bad. It's not as uncomfortable as I thought it would be. How do I look?"

"Beautiful."

As Bonnie slept, John watched her, even though it was a pitch-dark room. All he needed to see was the red light start flashing to show it was recording. He kept watching and waiting for it. The red light didn't come on to indicate it was recording but the dim green light did, so at least he knew his device was still connected to her brain. After an hour of no activity, he fell asleep too, with a high hope that it did work on everyone.

CHAPTER THREE

Every time John went to the bathroom, he checked the timer display showing only seconds added to it from the last time he checked. Either he needed to go to the bathroom more than usual, or his body just used it as an excuse to check. The alarm clock only had twenty minutes before it was about to go off and John was a little disappointed that the timer only read one minute fourteen seconds, nearly the same amount of time as Yüsli's. He was desperate to check to see what had recorded but knew the right thing to do was wait until she woke up. He purposely coughed to stir her a little. She slightly moved. He rolled over on his side, more forceful than normal, bouncing the bed. It worked. She stretched.

"Good morning."

"Huh?"

"Mornin', hun."

She opened her eyes and saw John's goofy expression on his face. "Oh, for Christ's sake already, watch the stupid thing, ya jerk."

Busted.

He removed it from her head, ejected the memory card and headed downstairs. He flipped the switch on the coffee pot and put the card in his computer. There it was, Bonnie's strange dream. *Yeah, she's even more demented than Yüsli is. I'm going to be rich!*

A half hour later, she came down the stairs. All John could do was smile. The still-angry Bonnie didn't even ask, purposely, and John knew she was waiting for him to.

He couldn't hold back any longer.

"So," John said, "I've watched your dream," with the image of the clown still paused on the screen.

"Uh huh," said Bonnie, pretending not to care. Although she was very curious, she didn't want it to show.

"Do you want to watch it?"

"Not right now, hun, I just woke up," she said, being stubborn, pouring a cup of the untouched coffee.

"Look, please stop being like this. You said that you wanted us to spend more time together. This is my life. This will be our life. I'm just trying to share with my beautiful fiancé, that's all."

Bonnie was a little embarrassed. She did want to spend more time with him, and yes, she was interested. After all, they were going to get married - eventually. *Why am I acting like this? What if this invention takes off, he becomes famous and leaves me?*

"Ok. You're right. I'm sorry. Go on, let's watch it. I don't even remember having a dream, so this should be interesting."

She sat by his side and rubbed his shoulder, staring into his eyes with sincerity. John smiled, kissed her soft lips, and played the video again.

Instead of watching the video, John watched her rub her forehead in embarrassment. After the short video ended, he had to ask. "So, what do you think? Your fear of clowns is obvious. See? I told you your dreams are more demented than Yüsli's."

"I don't think my dreams are usually this odd, though. Isn't it strange how this time the creepy clown has that gun? The same one, pointed at, wait, isn't that the same guy from the Yüsli's dream? And aren't dreams usually longer than a minute or so?"

"Don't know, hun. It's your dream. Yeah, the dream is a bit short, but I'm sure others will be longer. All of mine were. I think the reason the same gun and guy is in your dream is that you watched Yüsli 's with me. It probably just carried over to your dream, just like the KFC did with Yüsli's."

"I guess. That's just screwed up, though. Get in my mouth? Why would the clown tell you to get in his mouth? Why did the clown say Santiago at the end? How strange, but it's also very cool, John. Well done!"

"No one really realizes how strange their dreams are until they see them again. Most are forgotten by the time you wake up, but never again - with my dream machine," John said, already trying to compose a commercial. "The quality of the video will always be like this, regardless of your age, gender, or type of dream."

"Enough with the commercial, hun. I've already said it's pretty awesome. What are you going to call it? Maybe combine our names, Vogel and Anderson. Vogerson?"

"Um… Why should your name be first? I'm the creator. And we're getting married, so your last name will be the same."

"I'm keeping my last name, just hyphenating it. I told you that already. But what about Andervoge?"

"That's not a bad idea. 'The Andervoge.' It's kind of catchy. I'll think about it. When it's ready for release, I'll have made my decision."

The interest Bonnie now showed made John smile with pride. Bonnie completely changed her tune. "I'm sorry, I should've paid more attention to you. That was remarkable!"

John gloated from ear to ear. "Thanks."

"When will it be ready?"

"Technically I could release it right now, but I want to make sure it works on every single person. Just having it work on the three of us is a good sign, but I'd like to try it on a few more."

"Let's throw a dream machine party!"

"Hun, this device works when you're dreaming. Inviting people over for a party wouldn't work since you have to be asleep and dreaming for it to record anything. Plus, I only have one device, so inviting more than one person won't work either. One person at a time."

That's part of the problem, too. John didn't have friends. He was a huge geek in school, and the small number of friends he did have all went their separate ways and moved to different states, except for Yüsli. "Do you have anyone you can invite over? Maybe someone for tomorrow and someone else for Friday?"

"I guess so, but I have no idea how I'm going to explain this to my friends. Do they have to come over here? Can't we give it to them to wear at night, and have them give it back to us the next day?"

"I don't know about that, hun. I can't let this thing out of my sight. Not that anyone would steal it, or not give it back. And it's not that I don't trust your friends."

"Well, two of my friends coming here to sleep over would be extremely odd, too, don't ya think? I don't know any other way to present it to them."

John wasn't happy that he had to let his device leave the house, but he was so glad she turned over a new leaf. He hoped and prayed that his invention didn't cause long-term problems that are not apparent yet. It looks like this is going to become a reality.

*****

"John, this is Donna Cook. She works with me."

John extended his hand to greet Donna. He eyed every inch of her body and hoped it wasn't obvious he was looking for weapons. It's not like he could tell if she could be trusted or not just by looking at her, but what other choice did he have? If he's going to lend out this device he's worked on for the past ten years, he has to be sure it's going to be in good hands. His stress eased a bit knowing that he stuck a TrackR Bravo tracking device to the inside frame.

"When you go to bed tonight, just push this joystick." John showed Donna the secret method of turning it on and immediately regretted doing so. *At least I can change the code if I need to.* He then explained all about the lights and what they meant, not realizing she wouldn't be able to see them since she's the one who'd be wearing it.

"Please bring it back tomorrow morning, ASAP."

"That's all there is to it?" Donna questioned.

"That's it."

Donna turned the device over and over in her hand, several times, and admired the sleek design. "This is 100% safe, right?"

John, obviously concerned, looked at Bonnie. She quickly responded for him. "John's been using it for years and he's normal, ain't ya, hun?"

"Depends on what your definition of normal is."

Donna hugged Bonnie and thanked them both. "I'll see you both tomorrow morning."

When Donna got into her car, John feared he'd never see his device again. *What if she doesn't give it back? What if she breaks it? This thing is worth millions!*

CHAPTER FOUR

Donna's dream was the lengthiest so far. The timer showed a whole four minutes twelve seconds.

"Thank you, Donna," said John, already rudely ushering her towards the door. She looked back over her shoulder and said "Ok, then, I guess I'll see you tomorrow, Bonnie."

Donna hadn't even made it to her car when John asked Bonnie to watch it with him.

She knew what he did was rude but didn't mention it simply because she also knew her fiancé was super excited. Even though she had loads of stuff planned, she shared the moment with him. The dream was the strangest dream John had ever seen.

Visit www.bryankollar.com/donna.html
to view Donna's dream

"Look, there's that guy again," said Bonnie, pausing it at the very end of the video when he made his appearance.

"I don't understand. Donna hasn't seen the other dreams, how would she know about this man? I'll check into this. At least this one was over four minutes, not like the others which were all under two minutes. I can't charge $100 for under two minutes, can I?"

They watched the entire four-minute video and found it ridiculous that the famous sponge who lived in a pineapple under the sea, was murdered in cold blood by his boss, all because he started a rumor about a new product he created, the Krusty Dog.

"You know, Donna watches this cartoon every day with her kids. I bet you that's why she had a dream about this. It's strange how Mr. Crabbs was the one who committed murder, but not surprising that the creepy guy killed Mr. Crabbs. And then that name again. Santiago. Who is this Santiago guy they keep mentioning? That creepy guy's name is Billy, according to my dream, and Yüsli's, too, come to think of it."

"I have no idea," John said, shaking his head and dismissing it immediately. He was too excited and changed the subject, "Well, four for four success rate. I think I should now go public. I'm too excited and can't wait any longer."

"Wait, you told me to get two people, one for tonight and one for tomorrow. I already asked Isabella, another co-worker, to try this tonight. Should I call her to cancel?"

"Oh," John said, hoping this would be his first paying customer, "Think she'll pay?"

"Hun, don't be so greedy. I already told her we're asking for volunteers. She's more than excited and desperately wanted to do this last night, but she already had plans."

"Okay, but if all goes well, then we'll get started immediately."

*****

24

"Isabella, this is John Anderson, my loving fiancé. John, this is Isabella Grace."

John extended his hand. Isabella looked frightened and didn't extend hers. There was no smile on Isabella's face. Something wasn't right about her actions. He retracted his hand.

Without warning, she blurted out "I need you to promise me that I get to watch it first, in private."

"Excuse me?"

"My dream. Whatever gets recorded, I must see it first."

John looked at Bonnie in confusion. Bonnie saw Isabella's hands start to tremble.

"And if I don't like what I see, you don't get to watch it either," she continued.

A tad forceful statement to someone she never met, but it was right to the point. John disliked her immediately and wanted to punch her right in the face.

"I'm sorry, I can't agree with that. What gives you the right to demand something like that? This is my house, my invention!"

Bonnie grabbed Johns hand and spoke softly in his ear. She knew something wasn't right as this wasn't Isabella's usual bubbly self. "Isabella was telling me that ever since her husband went missing, she's been having terrible nightmares. She doesn't remember a thing about her dreams, but every night since he went missing, she keeps waking up, drenched in sweat, screaming."

John returned his stare to Isabella.

"Tell me why you have to watch the dream first." John's tension did not let up.

"Because that's how I want it. And I'm willing to pay you $2,000 if you respect my wishes."

Isabella grabbed the stack of banded cash from her front jean pocket and tossed it onto the nearby coffee table to make a statement and show how serious she was.

Bonnie never saw this side of Isabella before and wasn't sure she liked it.

"Do we have a deal? You can't watch the video unless I say so?"

"If you calm your attitude down a few notches, maybe," John said, even though his decision was already made up, staring at the cash on the table. He casually picked it up and just held it in his hand. It felt so good that he had to wrap his fingers around the stack of green paper.

"So… Let's get started."

"Wait, what? Right here? Right now?"

"Well, yes," Isabella said as if it were the strangest question she ever heard. "I've stayed up ever since Bonnie told me about this to make sure I can fall asleep without a problem. These nightmares make me go crazy, and I can't handle the added stress of wearing this device and being alone at the same time. Do you have somewhere I can sleep? I don't care if it's a pull-out couch. I'm extremely tired."

She was in a rush, alright. What the heck is going on? Why doesn't she want anyone to see it first? Is she acting this way because of being overtired?

"Excuse us for a moment," Bonnie said. She pulled John into another room to have a discussion, wad of cash still in his hand.

"What's up with your friend?"

"She's usually not like that," Bonnie said. "I've never seen that side of her before. I don't know. Maybe she's just terrified of what's going to be on the video?"

"Well, if her dreams are so scary, I would have thought that she would want everyone to view it together, wouldn't you?"

"I would've thought so." Bonnie glanced over her shoulder and saw Isabella pacing and turned back toward John. "She's drenched in sweat every night, John. I'm a bit concerned."

"Well, this I can't wait to see."

"But, John, you heard her. If you give her your word, you can't go back on it. If she ever finds out, I'm the one who works with her. I'll be the one to put up with all the drama."

Sigh.

John still held on to the cash tightly. It felt like new bills. *Is this real cash?* He looked at Bonnie. "Ok. So what do you think? Should we do this?"

Nothing needed to be said. Bonnie looked down at the floor and was just about to answer when there was a knock at the door.

"Make a decision yet?"

She's annoying.

"Ok. We'll do it your way."

"Remember, I want to watch it alone first."
Yes, I know, just shut up already!

Bonnie made up the guest room bed while Isabella impatiently stood behind her, waiting for her to finish. As soon as Bonnie tucked in the sheet and fluffed the pillow, Isabella sat down. "Thank you for understanding, Bonnie, I'm sorry."

"Isabella? I'm sorry for asking, but... are you on drugs?"

"Come on Bonnie, you know me. I never did drugs in my life!"

That's all that had to be said. Bonnie stared right into Isabella's sincere eyes. It was quiet for a few moments, so Bonnie finally replied. "I'm sure you have your reasons, Isabella. Where'd you get that kinda money?"

All Isabella could do was stare back. There was no response, and the silence was painful.

"Ok, well, John? I think she's ready."

John came in with his invention, and placed it on her head, still wanting to punch her in the face. Since she was ready, he just turned it on for her.

"Thanks for understanding, guys."
Huh? Did she say thank you?

"You're welcome," they both said at the same time.

Isabella pulled up the covers and switched off the light. Bonnie and John closed the door to the guest room, totally confused about what that was all about.

CHAPTER FIVE

The screams were horrible! She wasn't kidding when Isabella told Bonnie she woke up screaming and drenched in sweat every night. She had no idea it was to this extent! It was so unbearable that John and Bonnie had to wake her from her nightmare to make sure she was ok. *What could be that frightening? A migraine can't be this painful, can it?*

As soon as John entered the room, he immediately knew something was wrong. The smell of burning hair and flesh was his first sign. *Oh no, please, no!*

The timer showed six minutes, which is about the same amount of time they heard the horrid screams coming from their latest 'customer.'

John went to remove the device and let go immediately. It was hot to the touch. *Oh no! Was Bonnie right? Did this thing fry her brain?*

"What's going on, John," Bonnie asked, panic in her voice.

She touched the device too, and also let go, but then went right in and threw the device to the side, causing her hand to swell up almost immediately. Isabella's screams stopped instantaneously. She laid there, eyes wide open, staring at Bonnie in fear. John dialed 9-1-1.

While Bonnie rode in the ambulance with Isabella, John did what he promised not to do. Watch the video. He had no choice. Whatever dream she had caused his device to overheat making her scream in intense pain. If he went with them to the hospital and didn't know what was on that video, they'd probably question him about it anyway.

Since he had a huge obsession with his invention, his excuse to watch it now was because he feared he'd be out of business. If someone else had a nightmare as bad as she did, they could die. He no longer cared about the $2,000 payment and was pretty sure there would be a lawsuit over what happened, most likely costing him a lot more money than a measly two grand.

He ejected the memory card, still intact, thankfully, and put it into his computer. He took a deep breath, afraid of what he was about to see. *Nothing can be that horrifying!* He braced himself, took a deep breath, and pushed play.

*****

What he viewed was horrifying, but not that scary. Not enough to make someone scream the way she did. But now he understood why Isabella wanted to watch this first, alone. If what he was viewing actually took place, he knew there wouldn't be a lawsuit. Better yet, he knew he would get to keep that $2,000. Possibly get more out of her. A lot more. The dream showed Isabella killing her husband, the brutal hit to the head with a hammer, the points of contact of the blood splatter on the walls, then the kicks to the stomach, and finally, the location where the body was about to be dumped. The video ended

30

a bit short since the device was yanked off her head, so the area where the body would be, if this were real, could easily be found. There wasn't anything strange in this video like there was in every other dream he saw. This one looked like it was a crystal clear footage of a real murder, caught live on high definition camera. *Is this why her husband went missing? Does she keep having nightmares about her killing him? But why was she screaming the way she was?* For the first time, that creepy guy was nowhere in this video like he was in the others. *There's something more to this.*

The sound of the ringing phone startled John. It was Bonnie calling.

"Hun, I think you better come to the hospital. She's in intensive care, and the doctor has questions that I refuse to answer without you being here."

Sigh. Uh oh. "Hun, I have something to tell you."

"Can it wait until you get here? She's pressuring me."

"No, it can't. I watched the dream."

"What?!?! John, how could you?"

"What choice did I have? You heard the screams. I had to find out what was so horrible. I've never heard screams like that."

A man's voice was heard in the background talking to Bonnie. "Is your husband coming in?"

"Yes, doctor, just let me have a private conversation with him. He's leaving now."

31

She focused back on John. "John, get over here, please."

"But Bonnie, she may have killed her husband. I know where, how, and even the direction she drove to hide the body."

"Excuse me?"

"Her dream showed every blow, kick and almost the exact location the body may be. I'll bet you that's what her dreams are about, and those visions are coming back as nightmares."

"It's a dream, John. Both dreams you showed me had a murder, too."

"I'm 99% positive this one isn't like the others. It's vivid, real people, nothing strange happens in it at all, if you consider murder not being strange. The thing I can't figure out is why she screamed the way she did. Yeah, it was scary, but not enough to make someone scream like that, could it?"

Bonnie took a few seconds to answer, "But what about how hot that thing was?"

"Maybe my device tapped into a different part of the brain, and since it was a real event, it sent off different brain wave patterns to record something else? I don't know! I must investigate immediately!"

"Not before you get over here. We'll discuss more when you arrive."

John took the memory card, put it in a protective plastic case and placed that in his coat pocket. He patted it for reassurance that it was there, and headed to the hospital.

CHAPTER SIX

"John, this is Dr. Ed Grant. He has some questions for you."

I'm sure he does.

"John," Dr. Grant said, "Can you tell me what happened?"

"I wish I knew," John said with obvious voice fluctuation.

"Your fiancé told me that Isabella wore an invention you've designed?"

"Yeah, but so did several other people including my wife and me!"

"Don't get all defensive, John," said the doctor, taking a step backward, both hands in the air. "Yeah, but I'm assuming no one has the metal plate in their head like she does."

"Oooh….," John sighed, with an idea already in mind on how to fix the problem, or worse case scenario, have people sign a contract if this continues this business. There was still hope.

"It seems that the metal plate heated up and caused intense pain. There's no damage, but there probably would be it was left on for just a few more seconds."

Isabella glared at Bonnie. She knew what was coming. "Doctor, can you leave us alone, please, I need to speak with Bonnie and John in private."

That's what the rush was all about. Isabella wanted to talk to them about getting her hands on the video. Dr. Grant nodded his head and left the room.

"Do you have my video?"

John looked at Bonnie. Bonnie nodded her head no, as to not mention he watched it.

"Isabella," John started to speak, and Bonnie was afraid as to what was about to unfold. She tugged on his sleeve as to say don't do it, but he continued anyway. "Does a hammer, a kick, and a rug mean anything to you?"

Not needing to say a word, Isabella's eyes said it all. "You promised me! How dare you watch it first! Just for that, I will be suing you for what this thing did to my head!"

"Oh really," John said sarcastically, "and then I'd be showing the police what is on this video."

"I don't care. It's a dream. Go for it." Isabella looked the other way out the hospital window. She pushed the button for the nurse.

John knew it wasn't a dream, and Isabella had to be guilty. He saw it in her mannerisms. Bonnie realized at this moment that John was right. "So if I go to the location I saw on the video, there will be nothing there, right?"

It was almost comical the way Isabella looked right back at John. The nurse came into the room. "Can I help you?"

"Never mind, false alarm, sorry."

The nurse left the room. It was now a stare-down between all three. Bonnie knew she lost a friend, and probably a co-worker as well.

"What are you talking about? The location for what?"

"The body, your husband. From your house, you took Gemini Street, then Hanover St, then Main Street. Should I continue?"

John was bluffing. That was the end of the dream because the device was yanked from her head.

"I'm done with both of you. Please leave."

"But, Isabella…"

Isabella put her hand up to stop talking, and with the other pushed the button for the nurse.

It was so uncomfortable in the room they were glad to do just that. On their way home, they had a slight argument if it should be reported or not. Bonnie wanted to. Heck, it was a possible murder! But John didn't want to, simply because if she sued him for what it did to her head, it could cost him a heck of a lot more, including his entire business. But then again, even if she did sue, would it be a problem because she'd be in prison? Would they find the body? Was it honestly just a dream? He didn't want to take the chance.

"Why would she even come to you if it were true and had dreams about it? Why would she want video proof?"

"I can think of a few reasons," John said, reaching into a bag of chips while driving home. "Maybe she doesn't know what she's dreaming about and wanted to see it for herself. Or maybe she thought the dream machine would make the dreams stop?"

"Or maybe," Bonnie said, reaching into the

same bag of chips, "she does know what she's dreaming about and wanted to see if the dream machine could pick up on what she did, which is why she also offered $2,000 for her to view it first."

"I like your reasoning better," John said, eating the last chip. "Whatever the reason is, we can't report this. We'll hold onto the video until needed if we even need it at all. From now on we'll have to have people sign a contract before using it. I bet you that the metal plate had everything to do with changing the way the dream machine worked. I have to do more research. Maybe if I can figure out why this one recorded an image of a real event instead of a dream, I'd be able to make a second device to record real events. Double income!"

"Wait a minute. Are you still planning on doing this? You almost killed Isabella."

"As long as they don't have a metal plate in their head, they'll be fine. No one will know about this incident. We'll be fine."

"The doctor knows, John."

"Look, what else can I do? I'm not giving up ten years of my life because of this mishap."

"Why not? I gave up to ten years of mine." Bonnie looked the other way.

CHAPTER SEVEN

"I think you're making a big mistake."

"Look, I've already explained this to you. We've tried this on multiple people. I'm sure the problem with Isabella happened because of the metal plate in her head. That's the only possible reason it could have heated up. Since she started to scream right when the dream began, now we'll know we have to monitor it more closely."

She knew John was right, and as long as their customers signed a contract first, there shouldn't be any liability or lawsuits. Shouldn't be.

Bonnie just shook her head in agreement, but still wasn't happy with the situation. John picked up the phone and made a call to the local newspaper quickly before he changed his mind. With not being prepared and doing this on the spot, he stumbled over his words as what he wanted the advertisement to say. A $200 charge to his credit card later, they promised to place his ad in the top left corner of tomorrow's newspaper, entertainment section.

"Better be up early tomorrow, you may get inundated with phone calls," said Bonnie, finally joking around again. John didn't know if she was sarcastic or serious. This time, it was John who shook his head.

*****

Seven a.m. the next day, the phone rang. John was already up, having coffee, with the newspaper opened to the page of his advertisement.

The Daily B

Saturday, March 3, 2018

Video Record Your Dreams

Do you have strange dreams? Sexy dreams? Dreams that you'd like analysed? Well now you can! John Anderson has created the worlds first video dream recorder named "Andervoge." See your dreams as you saw them, in high definition, regardless of what you remember the next morning, permanently burned to a DVD for playback. Make an appointment now! Call

He smiled when he looked down at his phone and didn't recognize the number that was already calling him at this early hour.

"Andervoge, how can I help you?"

"Yes, um, I saw the advertisement in the newspaper for the dream recording service. How much do you charge, please?"

"$100, no matter how long the dream is."

"Oh, that's a bit pricey," the voice said. "I'll think about it. Thank you."

"Wait," John said, trying to keep his very first customer, "But even if it's an hour, that's only 1.6 cents per minute."

"Are dreams ever an hour?"

"Well, um, some may be. I had a few that were over an hour. May I ask what were you looking to spend?"

"I don't know, maybe $25?"

Was Bonnie right? Is $25 all anyone would be willing to pay?

"Maybe I could do $75. Would you like to give it a try?"

"Nah, I'll call back later. Sorry." The phone went silent. He jotted down the phone number for later callback, if need be, just when the phone rang again. He smiled once again.

"Andervoge, how may I help you?"

"I hope I'm not calling too early. If possible, I'd like to get my dream recorded to video tonight. Can you explain how the process works?"

"Sure, thanks for calling. You'd visit my office here in Shavertown, PA, and sleep overnight in our lounge room," John said, even though they didn't have the lounge room set up yet. "Then when you awaken, I'll move your dream to a DVD."

"Are you going to watch the dream first?"

Uh oh. Not again. "Well, I have to when creating the DVD for you, sir," John said,

39

wondering if this was another murder-type dream.

"Hm... How much is it to do this?"

John hesitated. "$100, but if nothing is recorded, which is quite rare, there will not be any charge."

"Do you have tonight available?"

YES!!! YES!! "Let me check my schedule." John ruffled some papers on his desk to make it seem like he was checking.

"Yeah, I can fit you in tonight. What time would you like?"

"I usually go to bed around eleven p.m., if that's ok with you."

John's phone rang again while he was talking and couldn't help but do a victory dance. Bonnie saw him point to his phone indicating yet another call coming in.

"Eleven is fine. What's your name please?"

"Brad Adams."

"Okay, Brad, I got you down. Feel free to bring whatever you want to help you sleep better, for example, your pillows, night light or music."

After the appointment was scheduled, he checked his voicemail, and sure enough, someone else wanted to set an appointment. While checking that voicemail, another call came through. *Maybe I should charge more!*

It was at this point he realized he'd have to switch around his night and day schedule. He wouldn't be able to sleep while they did, just in case another incident happened. He also worried about them getting up in the middle of the night and leaving with his prized possession. He had no choice but to monitor them while they slept, the most boring job ever; however, if he can do one every night, that's $500 a week for a five-day span, or $2000 a month. Not too bad for doing nothing at all. The best part of this new extra income is he'd still be able to send out his eBay orders as a power seller every day which was, with Bonnie's income too, just about enough to pay all the bills. Since he worked from home doing that, it didn't matter what time the orders were packed up. If this kept up, they'd have a little extra money.

Bonnie was already in the process of converting their spare bedroom into what they would now call "The Lounge" in preparation for tonight. She still wasn't too happy about it, but the fight they had last night made her realize John isn't going to give up on this. She put away the clutter and added decorations. There wasn't much to be done. It just had to look more pleasant, comfortable, and 'not just like a room.' She had a feeling her husband's business wouldn't last that long, and the calls that came in were because it's something new and different.

The Lounge already had an entrance of it's own, which may be a good thing, or maybe not. John wouldn't have to escort someone through their entire home to get to it, which would be very unprofessional, but the door may also be a way of someone leaving with his invention. While Bonnie decorated the outside of

41

The Lounge with advertisements, John went to Lowes to get a keypad lock, controlled by Bluetooth. If he gave the customer the combination for security reasons and they try to get out with his invention, he can easily lock it back up with the app on the phone since he'd be monitoring them all night long.

By six p.m., everything was 100% ready. Security cam setup, lock installed, and decorations throughout the room made it look very inviting and not just like a spare bedroom. John continued to make reservations and was already booked 1.5 weeks in advance.

CHAPTER EIGHT

10:45 P.M., John sat by the window waiting for Brad's arrival. With his very first true customer about to arrive, it was a very exciting (and stressful) moment! Right on time, a VW Jetta Sport pulled up. Bonnie must have done a remarkable job with the decorations because Brad pulled right up to it. John stood at The Lounge door and waited for Brad to exit the vehicle, a little too eager.

"Hi, I'm Brad. I have an appointment for 11 p.m."

"Right this way," John said motioning him inside.

"I'm a little nervous," Brad said, entering the newly decorated room. "Oh, this is nice in here."

"Thank you," John said, "but no need to be nervous."

"So how does this work? What will I be wearing?"

John hesitated before bringing out the invention. He was a little nervous as well. "All you need to do is wear this while you sleep."

The Andervoge felt much lighter than Brad thought it would be. "It's beautiful."

"Keep in mind, when you get ready for bed, there's a security camera up there." John pointed to the Reolink Go cam in the corner of the room. "So if you need to get changed, you can use the bathroom. When you're ready for bed, just put this on. There's nothing more.

43

When you wake up, I'll know because I'll be monitoring your sleep," John said, not mentioning the real reason he'd be monitoring him – fear of theft, damage or brain explosions. "At that point, I'll collect payment, and mail you the DVD once it's ready."

"Oh. I can't take it home with me tomorrow morning?"

"Unfortunately not. It may take a while to convert and burn your dream to a DVD, depending on what was recorded."

"Oh," Brad said, sounding disappointed. "Ok. Well, let's go for it. I'm a little tired, which is why I've chosen this time of night. I'm usually in bed by eight p.m."

Something didn't seem right to John, but it was probably just his nerves. "Aren't you going to change into something more comfortable?"

"Nah, I'm good to go. Thanks."

This made John very nervous. Brad was wearing jeans. "Okay."

John activated The Andervoge and handed it to Brad. The lights lit up like they should, except they didn't turn green because it wasn't connected to his brain yet.

"When you're ready to put this on, these lights will turn green to indicate it's connected. I'm just letting you know if you see lights coming from it."

"Will they be too bright for me to sleep?"

"Shouldn't be, it wasn't for my previous customers," John said, trying to make it seem like Brad wasn't his first.

John locked the exit door with his phone, purposely in front of Brad, and John sensed Brad felt even more nervous than he was.

"In case of an emergency, the security code for the door is 5-3-1-2. I have to lock it for security reasons. Please keep in mind that it's Bluetooth controlled, so I can lock and unlock it with my phone if needed," John said, waving the phone back and forth.

Brad nodded.

"All that's left is to sign here," John said, handing him the first ever copy of the agreement, knowing that at some point it would be revised – again and again. "It's just a bunch of legal mumbo-jumbo."

Brad just glanced at it, and as most people do these days, signed it without reading anything.

"You're good to go. Good night. If you need me, just call for me. I can hear through the security camera. Feel free to use the TV if you want, and I'll see you in the morning, okay? Whenever you're ready to leave, no matter what time it is, let me know, I'll be awake."

Just as John was about to close the door, he thought of something else, making things up as the night goes on. He assumed it would be like this for the first few customers. "Oh, I forgot to mention. An alarm will sound at eight a.m. to wake you up. I'll give you a half hour to fully get situated, and then I'll be in to get you."

Brad sat on the bed and John exited the room using the entrance to the main house. Bonnie was waiting on the other side and gave him a high five. Their first customer!

The office monitor displayed everything the security cam was recording. The lights were already off and the night vision was incredible. All John had to do was stay awake until the newly designated eight a.m. time limit. He took a long swig of water from his Cirkul bottle. It was going to be a long night.

*****

They did it! Both Bonnie and John stayed awake all night, playing games, keeping each other active and alert. It sure seemed Brad was restless with the amount of toss and turns they witnessed and was surprised he got any sleep at all, but sure enough, the timer showed two minutes, which was still quite low compared to his dreams, but at least there wasn't any screams or smell of burning flesh.

Brad awoke at an early six a.m., and unlike most people do, got right out of bed, jolly and chipper. "Hello?"

"Yes, we're here."

"I'm ready to go now."

"Be right there."

John showed up in just seconds to greet Brad.

"Did I dream? I don't think I did."

John pointed to The Andervoge's timer.

"Yup. The timer shows here just slightly above two minutes."

Even though he felt guilty as hell for collecting $100 for just two minutes, that guilt quickly passed after he realized its $100 for seven and a half hours. He never factored in the time that he had to stay up and watch over everyone. *That's only $13 an hour. This isn't as profitable as I thought. But where else can you sit around and do nothing for $13 an hour?*

He collected payment with the Square reader from his phone and promised Brad a quick twenty four hour turn-around time. They shook hands, and Brad went home.

"Let's get some sleep. Do you realize we've been awake almost twenty-four hours? We got up at eight yesterday. I can't do this every night with you, I'm sorry, I have a day job."

"OK, but let me start converting this to DVD first. I'll be there in a minute."

John started playing the video and after a few seconds knew he would have to watch it in its entirety, even though it was so ridiculous and unbearable, mainly because this creepy guy was the main character of the entire dream. It stopped Bonnie in her tracks from going upstairs, too.

Visit www.bryankollar.com/brad.html
to view Brad's dream

She rubbed her forehead in confusion and couldn't take her eyes away from what she was seeing. She had to watch, just like people do with a bad accident on the side of a highway. She nudged John. "Um, hun? Why is this creep in every dream? I don't think your invention is working."

John was having doubts too but didn't want to accept it. "What the heck? That's odd. I don't know. I hope this device isn't altering people's dreams. I want pure results. I promise I'll look into it."

"Maybe," said Bonnie, unsure what to think about it. She laughed out loud when a very large can of soup held a gun to the creepy guy in the middle of someone's kitchen, commanding him to climb inside the soup can. "Now I've seen it all. This really can't be a dream, It's just too dumb. Can we go to bed now, please?"

"Sure." John put a blank DVD in the drive so it can automatically start to burn after the conversion process was complete, even though this two-minute video wouldn't take long at all. He was positive that something wasn't right. *Who is this guy?* These dreams were much shorter than his, but he used the excuse that maybe that's how long most people dream and he was an exception. Even though he felt very guilty, he had no intention of putting his business on hold. It was quick, easy cash. *Maybe these really are dreams?* He already had a plan in mind if questioned about it. The excuse he'd give is that he needed to use it on more and more people while he figured out what the problem was. A poor excuse, but there wasn't any reason someone would question it.

CHAPTER NINE

John and Bonnie awoke at twelve p.m with about six hours sleep. Waking up at twelve wasn't that bad as he thought, but he had a feeling some of his clients may stay right until the cut-off time, and some may leave a lot earlier, screwing up his sleep patterns. John had no choice to get used to a new sleep schedule, but it was going to be extremely difficult not being able to sleep next to his fiancé every night. Maybe if he built another one, or two, or even three, he could have a few people coming in all on the same day. He certainly had the time to make more while waiting for his clients to wake up. And three clients at the same time would bump that $13 an hour to $39 an hour. But then again, where would he fit everyone? They obviously can't all stay in the same room.

Their next appointment scheduled for ten p.m. didn't seem too far away. They had a quick lunch knowing that in a few hours they probably would be having dinner.

The local mail already arrived and John had to run to the post office to get Brad's DVD mailed. To save time, he got his Ebay orders packed up so it would be one trip. From now on, he'd tell his clients twenty-four to forty-eight hour turn-around time for their video to arrive in the mail. Another thing they didn't plan on is the change of bed sheets every day. So while John went to the post office, Bonnie went out to get four more, one for each day of the week. She also realized she has a new job as well – doing laundry every weekend.

Before they knew it, there was a knock at the door, 9:30, a little early. "Hi, I'm Jim Rinker, I have a ten p.m. appointment with The Andervoge."

"Come right in," Bonnie said. John shot her a look as if she was trying to take over his business.

John stepped in front of her and explained the same scenario as he did to Brad.

A few hours after Jim was under the sheets, he was still wide awake. John kept his eye on his customer while drawing up blueprints of how to make The Andervoge better with a new live feature he was contemplating. His freshly brewed pot of Meadow Ridge Coffee was his only hope of keeping him awake. Unfortunately, all Jim did was toss and turn.

"Everything ok?" said John through the security system.

"I can't seem to fall asleep in this room."

"Is there anything I can do to make you more comfortable?"

"No, it just takes time. I'll fall asleep eventually."

Eventually never happened, and Jim barely slept at all. All night long he tossed and turned, and the timer showed 00:28. The shortest amount of time ever recorded.

Bonnie was just about to leave for work while Jim was getting ready to leave. "We can't charge him for that, can we," John said as Bonnie was halfway out the door.

"Hun, I know you feel guilty. I would too," Bonnie said, in a rush to get out the door. "These aren't dreams. You know it, I know it. And yet, just yesterday, you told me you wanted to charge even more? I know it's difficult to accept. Even if in the smallest chance that they are dreams, you're up that entire time. They are getting a bargain. Now, I'm going to be late for work. You're going to have to make that decision on your own. It's your invention, you decide. Love you, bye!"

John watched Bonnie leave and waved to her out the window as she drove out of the driveway like they do every single day since they've been together. *I somehow have to let my customers know that the cost is $100 regardless simply because I have to stay up with them the entire time. I don't know. I'm sure this will get easier on me after each customer.*

"Sorry, Jim, we only got a twenty-eight-second video. I'm still going to have to bill you for it."

"No, I understand. Business is business. Can we schedule another one for tomorrow, please?"

Sweet! Customers don't mind!

"Sorry, I'm booked out until next week. How's Friday sound?"

"Next Friday, ten p.m. See you then."

John was pretty sure there wouldn't be anything worthwhile to convert over, but he did check it out.

Visit www.bryankollar.com/jim.html
to view Jim's dream

Sure enough, there he was again. This time, that creepy guy was the only person in the video, in women's makeup, saying *'Am I pretty'* over and over again, with the sound of a single gunshot at the end. He quickly dialed his wife.

"You're not going to believe this, hun. That short video clip? It's just that guy. The whole video was him, wearing makeup, asking if he was pretty."

"Oh my God, you're kidding me."

John stared at the paused image of the man with the horrible makeup job. "I think he shot himself at the end. Isn't that funny?"

"I'm sorry, hun, I can't talk right now. Traffic is horrible and I forgot my Bluetooth. I've given up on that device. I've told you before, and I'm only going to say it once more… You really shouldn't be charging anyone until you figure it out, but I know that's not going to happen. I'll see you when I get home, we'll talk about it then."

*****

A week went by. John now had eight customers so far but technically wasn't any more wealthy because he made a promise to himself. All the money he made should go to pay off the credit card first, the main reason he didn't want

53

to stop charging people. But the best part of this – no deaths. Still, the shortest dream was Jim's, who was scheduled to come back in two days, and the longest dream was now thirty-seven minutes. Even though John was extremely concerned that every single dream had this guy in it with the same gun, it wasn't doing anybody any harm (other than technically stealing from people by knowing that these were not dreams.) It was a bit eerie, but also amusing at the same time. The strangest thing of all was the content of the dreams, each one seeming weirder than the previous, but yet no one questioned him on the validity of it all. No one even mentioned the creepy guy because people dream of other people they don't know all the time.

As long as his customers didn't request to watch the other dreams, which they had no reason to, they'd never know this man was in every single dream. Every moment of his spare time (which was quite a lot because of waiting for his customers to awaken) was trying to figure out what was going on. *What does this all mean? Who is this man in every dream? And that gun…*

John truly felt he had no choice. He had to continue. He had to see what would unfold next and was not about to give up ten years of his life. *Don't charge him!* That's the exact thought that ran through his mind as he placed it on his customer every night. And then he thought *I'm going to go to Hell for this* when he made up his mind to charge him anyway, thinking of how quickly that credit card balance is coming down.

*****

The weekend had now arrived and was a special day for John. His good Facebook friend, Adrian Chiang, flew all the way in from Singapore to hang out with him. John cleared his schedule for an entire week so they could hang out together.

The sole purpose of Adrian's visit initially was to hang out and didn't have anything to with The Andervoge, but when John asked him to try it, Adrian was anxious to give it a whirl. On the second night of his vacation, they gave it a go, hoping to get more every night before he heads back home.

Knowing that Adrian was a gamer, the dream did relate to an ever popular online video game, so John had high hopes that maybe the device was working after all. Unfortunately, the first attempt was only forty-six seconds.

Visit www.bryankollar.com/adrian.html
to view Adrian's dream

The dream was all about the popular Minecraft game, green creepers and all. For the first time, there wasn't any visual of a gun or shooting in this dream. But Mr. Creepy did appear for a second or two, and John did hear the name Santiago again. *Why is Creepy Billy guy saying the name Santiago?*

55

Between clients and while Bonnie was at work, he made modifications to The Andervoge in hopes that Billy wouldn't be in every dream. Although unsuccessful, he was proud that he was able to finish the 'live mode' modification to his device. From now on, he would be able to view the video feed 'live' as it was recording. And, instead of converting it to a DVD, he just moved the video to a flash drive, which a request by most of his customers.

Today was the first time he'd use the live viewing process, but also today, his sleep schedule would be thrown completely off, all because of Nigel Lee, this morning's customer, who sleeps during the day due to his third shift job.

It was a bright and early morning when Nigel arrived around nine a.m, which is about the time John was usually heading off to bed.

Although the instructions were almost the same, they had greatly expanded from what he told his first customer. When Nigel fell asleep, the dream started to record. John was able to watch it, live, as Nigel dreamt it, using the built-in tiny 2-inch monitor attached to The Andervoge, and also on a large 50-inch monitor on John's desk. He wished Bonnie was here right now to share this experience of his new modification, even though she no longer wanted any part of it. He rushed over to his big screen monitor to get a better view. There, in Nigel's dream, was Mr. Creepy. Something was different already. This time, it seemed like Nigel was focusing on nothing but Billy way back in the distance. Nothing but mist engulfed Billy. It looked as if the video was coming from the eyes of a predator, sneaking up his prey, quickly getting closer and closer to him. Something wasn't right, but he kept watching for what would happen next. Once nothing but Billy's face completely engulfed the screen, he smiled, bearing razor sharp teeth. Billy said "**Tag, you're it**," followed by a bright flash of light.

John fell over backward in his chair and collapsed to the floor.

CHAPTER TEN

Um…. Where am I? John opened his eyes to find himself standing somewhere. Just where he wasn't sure. Either he was in a dream state himself, or somebody took him somewhere while he was passed out. All around him was nothing at all. No walls, no life forms of any kind, no sun or moon, no sky, no earth, nothing. It looked like a million miles of empty nothingness, with just a misty, glowing haze floating above his feet. *Do I have feet? Is there a ground?* John was afraid to move for fear of having no feet. He slowly took a step and didn't fall through the nothingness. *Am I in Heaven?* The only sounds he heard was what sounded like Darth Vader's breathing and a single beep every second or so.

"Hello? Anyone there?" No answer, except an echo of his voice that made it sound like if he were in the largest endless warehouse in the world. The sound of the constant annoying breathing was persistent. He continued to walk, slowly, and more confidently with each step he took, even though he didn't feel anything solid under his feet.

Assuming this had to be a dream, he walked normally, but still cautiously. If this somehow wasn't a dream and there was a huge gaping hole to fall into just inches away, he'd never see it.

He called out again. "Hello?" No response.

"What the heck! Hello? Anyone?" *I have to be dreaming! At least I'll have it on video if I'm wearing The Andervoge.*

The only choice he had was to continue walking. This place had to end somewhere. He looked at his watch. 7:25 p.m. *How long have I been walking? A half hour?* He placed his hand in his back pocket. *My cell phone! It has a signal!*

He dialed Bonnie, she answered on the first ring. "John! I've been trying to call you. Where are you?"

"I don't know. There's nothing here."

"What do you mean nothing here? What do you see?"

"Nothing! Not a thing except a slight mist floating from the floor. I don't see a road, a ceiling, any obstacles, people, a sky! Nothing!"

"What? John, are you ok?"

"No! I'm terrified. What's going on?"
"Text me a picture of where you're at, hun."
John took a photo of what he thought was nothing, but the preview of the image knocked him on his ass, dropping his phone into the mist.

From a sitting position, and now in panic mode, John felt around the mist, his hand moving rapidly in search of his phone. When he finally found it, he pushed send. The phone beeped and displayed "Low battery warning – cannot send photo. Please charge now."

"Oh no, Bonnie, I can't send a photo. It looks like my phone is about to die, but I saw a shadow image of someone in my photo!"

"Do you have a charge cable with you?"

"Hun, listen to me. Even if I did, I can't plug it in. There's NOTHING HERE. Don't you understand? NOTHING. I'm in a huge empty place with nothing around me!"

"No, I don't understand. There has to be something there. What are you talking about?"

John was frustrated, as his battery flashed red. "DAMN. I can't, hun. There's nothing to explain, and my battery is going to run out. I have to conserve as much battery as possible. Please, call the police. Have them ping my cell phone and track where I am. I estimate I have about fifteen minutes of battery life if I don't use the phone. I have to go."

John didn't want to, but he hung up without waiting for a response. He had to. Every second of saving battery counts. His only means of communication with his fiancé and he had to disconnect the call. He wanted to take another photo to see what else he can capture but was too frightened, and that would only drain his battery drastically.

Wherever he was, he was still getting a cell phone signal, so felt that was positive. He quickly disabled wireless, Bluetooth, and turned the screen brightness all the way down. It was dark in this place, except for the faint white glow coming from the mist underneath him. If he needed to see his phone, he would have no problem. He continued to walk, very anxious now knowing that someone else is there with him.

"Hello," he said again. "I know someone is there!" He wanted to look at the photo again, but every single second of phone use means less battery power. The annoying Darth Vader breathing was getting more irritating by the second, but remained at a constant volume, no matter how far or in which direction he walked.

John checked the time again. 8:46 p.m. *I've been walking for over an hour! When will I get somewhere? Am I actually moving? Is time doubled? Tripled?* He kept trudging along, not even feeling a bit tired or sore. *What happens if I have to go to the bathroom? Where do I do it?* He hoped that he wouldn't need to go until he got to where he was going, wherever that may be.

Finally, silence! The sound of the Darth Vader breathing ceased to exist. What a relief! But that 'every second beep' changed to an annoying constant beep. *What the heck is that?* Seconds later, the constant beep sound stopped, resumed its every-second beep, and then the Darth Vader started again. *Sigh.*

3:43 a.m., John finally gave up. Nothing had changed. His surroundings were identical from the moment he arrived and now was pretty sure he wasn't walking, even though his legs were moving. He sat down, on nothing, bored out of his mind and pondered. *I'm not tired, but it's pointless to walk any further!* He brought out his phone. 1% battery power. The time on his phone matched his watch.

A second Darth Vader sound came out of nowhere, followed by another second-by-second beep.

"Hello! Someone! Anyone! Is someone else there? PLEASE!"

"Hi," replied a very familiar voice.

CHAPTER ELEVEN

"Yüsli?"

"Yeah! John? Is that you? Where are you?"

"I don't know! Where are you?"

"I don't know either. There's nothing around here. It's just a vast wide…"

"I know, I know," John interrupted, excited that he may get out of this situation. "Keep talking. We'll follow each other's voice."

"Um, ok. What is this place? How long have you been here?"

John started to walk but couldn't figure out from which direction Yüsli's voice was coming.

"Probably about eight hours, if time is ticking by like it is supposed to." John turned around and asked Yüsli a question. "What about you?"

"I don't know. Just now I woke up on this cloud of mist." Yüsli's voice wasn't coming from any direction in particular.

"I don't know where to go," John said, now just standing there. "No matter which direction I turn, your voice sounds the same. Can you get to me?"

"I'm afraid to walk, John. There's a cloud under me. Is this safe?"

"Yes, Yüsli, It's safe. As I said before, I've been walking on it for hours. Let me guess. You have no clue as to how you got here too, am I right?"

"No idea. What the hell is going on?"

"Wish I knew!"

They spoke for what seemed to be hours. Neither of them was a bit tired, hungry, or had to go to the bathroom. At least they were no longer bored to death since they could talk to each other. It took them only a few minutes to realize they had the same story.

Yüsli finally asked the question he was afraid to ask from the start. "Are we dead?"

"Probably. That's why nothing is around us."

"Did your Andervoge kill us?"

"I don't think so… I mean, I don't even remember wearing it. Do you?"

"Except for that time you put it on me, no, I don't think so. I'm not sure."

"Well, we're both here. At some point, we both wore the thing. I've been wearing it on and off for ten years. Why didn't I get here sooner? And why did you arrive now instead of ten years later? This doesn't make any sense. I wonder if everyone I used it on is here or on their way. Maybe I haven't walked far enough to hear their voice? Maybe we're all in a parallel world? I bet ya that person it nearly killed screwed up my invention."

"Um, it nearly killed someone? Was this before or after you used it on me?"

"Long story."

"It seems like we have time."

John didn't answer, and Yüsli was now nervous but shook it off. He knew he'd get it out of him at some point. "I tell you what, even after just four hours of this crap, I'd rather be dead. How long is this going to go on?"

John started to walk again. He could either sit there and be bored or keep walking since he doesn't get tired. *Maybe I found Yüsli by walking. Maybe I'll find someone else to talk to as well. Maybe I can figure this whole thing out if I just keep walking.*

The entire time John walked, so did Yüsli, or at least he said that's what he was doing. Each other's voice remained the same volume.

"Are we just walking in circles since we technically can't see where we're going," Yüsli asked knowing that John wouldn't have an answer.

"Probably. But if we're going to be bored, we may as well keep walking. Look, we found each other, let's find the others."

"We don't even know if there are others! How many miles have you walked?"

"How would I know? I do know I've been walking for at least ten hours straight and I'm not even tired. How's that possible? I don't need to take a break, so I may as well do something."

Sure, John wasn't tired, but he certainly was bored. With neither of them being a good conversationalist, they couldn't keep a conversation going for more than five minutes at a time. The boredom was getting to both of them. The persistent sounds of two Darth Vader's breathing and those annoying beeps were already being subconsciously blocked out.

As John continued to walk, his foot hit something solid. This something slid across the 'floor' making a metal scraping sound. *Metal? Against what? Mist?*

"Yüsli! My foot hit something solid."

"Excuse me? What did it feel like?"

"I don't know. I kicked it, not touch it."

John got on his hands and knees. Felt around the mist, hand going through nothing." *How am I not falling through this nothingness?* The farther he reached down, the deeper his hands went – underneath his feet. He stood back up and started to walk slowly again, losing all the confidence he had before. He swished his foot in a back and forth motion. *Clunk.*

"There it is again! What the heck could that be clunking off of?"

He swished his foot around once more, wide swipes, slowly. When it hit the object again, he reached down and grabbed it.

Photo courtesy of Midnight Tactical

"Um, Yüsli? It's a gun!"
"What??! A gun?"

CHAPTER TWELVE

"The very first solid object in this place! Why would there be a gun here? It looks like the gun from everybody's dreams."

"It's a sign," Yüsli said. "What, I don't know, but it's a clue!"

"It's a sign, alright," John said. "Maybe it's meant for me. Maybe I'm supposed to kill myself to get back to the real world."

"No, it's not meant for you to kill yourself. Isn't it obvious what you're supposed to do with it? Just shoot it, see what happens."

John checked the chamber. "It only has three bullets, Yüsli. I'll just try it once." He aimed at nothing at all and had a concern that if he shot into nothing, it would somehow hit Yüsli. Anything was possible in this strange situation.

He pulled the trigger anyway. The bullet made an audible whizzing sound as it exited the barrel. Three seconds later, the whizzing sound was heard once again when he felt the bullet whisk by his right shoulder. Startled, he quickly moved to his left when the sound of the bullet whizzed by yet again after three more seconds. He kept moving to his left, but he felt the bullet breeze by no matter how far he moved.

"Yüsli! I can hear and feel the bullet pass my right shoulder every three seconds! It's in an endless loop! What have I done!"

"Well, move to your left!"

"Don't you think I've already tried that? No matter how far I move, I still feel it whisk by."

It was to the point where the bullet now went by at least fifteen times and still was as strong as the first.

"Yüsli, I think I'm on to something here. This has to be why we're not going anywhere when we walk. If the bullet keeps passing my right shoulder, I must be in a tiny vortex type room."

"But why do you still feel it whip by you even when you move to the left? What happens when you move to the right?"

"The bullet would finally make an impact, probably."

"I don't think so," Yüsli said. "When we walk, we're probably not even moving, no matter what direction we think we're turning."

It made sense, to a point. He was sure this had to be the reason he wasn't going anywhere when he walked for hours. *I can't possibly be moving. But why is the bullet whisking passed me, over and over again?*

Frustrated beyond belief, he went for it. He moved ever so slightly to the right. The bullet still whizzed by, the same location. He moved once again, quite a bit to the right. No change. Without giving it any thought, he placed his hand in the location where the felt the bullet passing him.

"Ouch! Damn!!"

"Are you ok?"

The pain was unbearable! The bullet went right through his hand, but three seconds later, the pain was completely gone. The sound of the bullet was slightly slower. How that was possible was even more impossible than the situation they were in.

"The bullet slowed down, Yüsli, I can sense it. I'm pretty sure my hand slowed down the bullet a little."

"I'm so sorry I suggested it. So your shoulder didn't get hit, your hand did?"

"Yeah. I put my hand out to see what would happen."

"Well, that was stupid. Why aren't you still screaming?"

John looked at his hand. Perfectly normal. No blood, no hole through it, nothing, as if it never happened, but yet the bullet kept whizzing by.

"Why do you keep asking me questions you know I can't answer," John snapped and soon after felt sorry but didn't apologize.

"The only way to prevent this bullet from consistently passing me is to stop it. And it seems the only way to do that is let it impact something to slow it down. And the only thing it could impact is my body. I can't take the risk of letting it hit my head, although it may be fine three seconds later like my hand is, I can't take that risk."

"So, you're going to keep blocking it with your hand until it slows down completely, aren't you."

"What choice do I have?"

There was nowhere to brace for impact, but John was ready. He clenched his teeth and put his hand out again. Sure enough, the pain was as bad as the first time but also vanished again just like before. He watched his hand seal itself up immediately, right before his eyes. The sound of the bullet wasn't as strong as before, too.

"I think it's working, Yüsli. I'm going to have to deal with the pain. It only lasts a few seconds, but I got to stop this bullet."

Each of the 20 times the bullet hit, there was less and less pain. Finally, there wasn't enough force for it to go through and he was able to catch it in his hand.

Photo courtesy of Midnight Tactical

"It's over, Yüsli. I finally got the bullet. What the hell is going on?"

"Wish I knew."

"So now what?"

"Really, John? Come on. What the heck do you think," he snapped. "There's nothing we can do. Nothing. Absolutely freakin' nothing. This is horrible. I'm extremely irritated. I'm bored out of my mind. I have two choices. I can walk or stand here. I'm wide awake. I can't fall asleep."

Yüsli was either stressed, or the mist of smoke coming from beneath his feet was poisonous. John felt the same level of stress, maybe more, but he wasn't letting it show for Yüsli's sake. The rant continued again. "If I were able to sleep, I'd do that the entire day or night, or whatever the heck it is, just for something to do. I am going insane! There's no use walking, you proved that and shattered my hope for rescue."

Yeah, like it's all my fault. John let the comment go. "We probably are going somewhere when we walk. I mean, I know I was at least moving my feet as if I were walking for at least ten hours, and I'm sure I would've kicked that gun at some point sooner if I were at a standstill. And then you didn't show up until six hours after I started walking, so maybe walking helps. Here, let's do a test. Now that I have something solid, I'll put this down. I'll walk for two seconds. I'll reach down, and see if it's still there. That will prove if I'm going anywhere."

"Good idea! But what if you go to grab it and it's not there? Maybe we'll need it later?"

"To kill what? There's nothing here," this time John snapped until he remembered the photo he took on his phone. There was no way of explaining it to Yüsli because he wasn't even 100% sure what he saw, and he didn't want to frighten him or get him any more upset.

He carefully placed his hand down in the mist, ready to let go of it. He took his hand off it, and immediately put it back down. It was still there. He stood up and crouched back down. Still there. He walked two steps and felt for the gun. It was gone! He felt all over the mist and felt nothing.

"What the hell, Yüsli, I didn't even go anywhere! I took two steps! What is going on! The gun is gone!"

CHAPTER THIRTEEN

It sure was difficult to feel around the floor without a floor being there. It was so very strange how he was able to touch the bottom of his sneakers while searching for the gun.

"I'm walking on nothing, Yüsli. I can feel the bottom of my sneakers but yet I'm floating on air. I bet that gun didn't float, it fell to… somewhere."

"You should have tried that with your sneaker, John."

John kept walking, swishing his feet in wide strides the entire time, hoping to kick either that gun or something else that would help solve this mystery.

It's a good thing no one can see me. I must look like a fool doing this.

"Yüsli, are you doing anything to help this situation?"

"What do you mean? What the heck am I supposed to do?"

"Anything. Search the ground for objects, maybe? What are you doing?"

"Just standing here."

John was frustrated. Sure, there wasn't much to do, but Yüsli standing there really ticked him off.

"Do I have to explain every step to you as a child? Start walking! Search for items on your hands and knees, or swish your feet around. If a gun was here, I'm sure we'll find something else. How can you possibly do nothing?"

Yüsli let out a sigh which made John even angrier.

"Fine, forget it. I'll be the one to get out of this place, and you'll be stuck here forever."

"Alright, alright," Yüsli said, now sounding irritated too.

After a full eight minutes of walking like fools, swishing their legs, the sound of something skidded across the mist in front of Yüsli.

"You're right, John, I kicked something!"

"A gun?"

"No, I don't think so, although it felt just as heavy."

Yüsli got on his hands and knees and did the feel thing. "This is kinda creepy, John, there's nothing under my feet or hands."

John sighed. "Where have you been this entire time? That's what I've been trying to explain to…"

"Found it," Yüsli interrupted. He lifted the item from the mist.

"Um, looks like I won't go hungry if I ever do get the munchies."

"You found food? What is it?"

"A KFC bucket with loads of chicken."

"Stop it. You're joking, right?"

"No, John. Looks like the same bucket I had that night you came over."

"What the heck is that doing here?"

"Smells fresh and it's still hot. Oh, and look, there's the sticker on the side of the tub. It has last weeks date!"

"What. The. Heck. Is. Going. On! Is there anything else near it?"

No response, except for the sound of lip smacking and finger licking.

"You're eating it, aren't you, Yüsli."

"Give it a break, John, I told you. I'm incredibly bored. I get to do something other than walk around. Maybe later I'll have the excitement of being able to go to the bathroom."

Even though John was a bit jealous, he probably would have done the same thing.

"Is there anything else there?"

"I don't know. Give me a minute. I'm eating. I got all the time in the world. I'll search later. This stuff is good! Why would a bucket of chicken be here?"

Sigh. John continued to swish his foot around again until a thought crossed his mind as to why the bucket of chicken might be there.

"Yüsli, I just thought of something. Did I ever tell you what your dream was about?"

"No, but I wouldn't doubt it has something to do with this delicious chicken."

"Colonel Sanders, the chicken guy, pointed a gun at someone, making him drive him to KFC. He forced him to get the whole thing on video. When they didn't have what he wanted in the drive-thru, he blew up the KFC building."

"Hmm… So this bucket of chicken came from my dream? Are we stuck in my dream and can't get out because I'm not dreaming anymore?"

"That's the most sense you've made this entire time. It's possible, I guess. That would explain the vast emptiness of this place. If we're in your dream, then there are even more questions. Why are we still in it when your dream happened about a week ago? How did I get here? I don't think I was wearing The Andervoge. How did you get here when you haven't worn it since then? What's happening in the real world? Most importantly, how do we get out?"

CHAPTER FOURTEEN

The tears finally stopped flowing from Bonnie's eyes. It's not that she wasn't sad any longer, it's just that she could no longer cry.

"Thanks for visiting, Donna. The doctor still has no idea what's going on. Neither one of them is in a coma. Look at their eyes," Bonnie said, pointing to John, then Yüsli, both in their hospital beds. "They are moving back and forth as if they are both dreaming. And look at their legs. Both of them are slightly moving them as if they are walking. John's legs were going for hours just moments ago."

"So what were you going to tell me about their oxygen masks?"

"Oh, yeah. If we take someone's oxygen mask off, they struggle to breathe. Then the machine sounds an alarm with a constant beep as if they flatlined, but yet that same machine shows a normal heartbeat. The doctor confirmed it's not faulty equipment and never seen this happen before. We have that on as a precaution."

"They sound like Darth Vader," Donna said, smiling at Bonnie, trying to lighten things up. When there was no response, not even a smile, she continued. "Hey, don't worry, I'm sure the doctors will figure it out." Even though Donna said it with a positive attitude, the look in her eye showed hopelessness.

The silence and energy in the room was horrible. Donna kept trying to change that energy around by talking and asking questions.

"So you just found John flat on his back? Don't you have security cameras? Can't you pull the footage to see what happened?"

"Yeah, they were set up, but only in The Lounge so he could watch over his clients. John has no signs of any scratches, bumps, bruises or even a struggle. Isn't that strange?"

"What about Yüsli? That's his name, right? You can't blame yourself for what happened to him." Donna finally slid a metal chair along the floor and placed it next to Bonnie. The horrible screech sound it made was almost enough to wake up John and Yüsli from the state they were in. She sat down and put her hand on Bonnie's lap."

"I tried to call Yüsli, several times, but he wasn't answering his phone. Since this was an urgent issue, I went to his residence, and there he was. Same scenario. His chair had fallen over, and Yüsli was flat on his back, too, gasping for breath, just like I found John."

"You probably got there right in the nick of time."

With the foot-tapping sound of Donna's leg bouncing up and down and the extremely pale complexion on her face, Bonnie knew what was running through Donna's mind.

"Hey," Bonnie said, looking at Donna right in the eyes trying to reassure her safety. "I'm sure you're going to be ok. If The Andervoge did cause this, maybe it just doesn't work properly on men."

83

"That's not too reassuring, Bonnie. Stop trying to bullshit your way out of this. You know as well as I do that I'm in danger, and probably all the others who have worn this. Have you contacted anyone else who wore this thing?"

"I wish I could," Bonnie said, now with the same white complexion. "I've searched for John's records, but he never was good at bookkeeping. I wore it before you did, so I'm the one who would be next."

"Well, what about his last customer? If John was flat on his back, did that customer pick up and leave?"

"Yeah. That security footage showed his customer calling for John many times before finally giving up. He left The Advervoge on the bed, along with a note, and exited the room using the security code John gave him."

"What did the note say?"

"Just six words. *I'm not happy. Call me.* No phone number, nothing else."

Both of them sat there in the hospital room with the TV on for background noise, flipping through channels and stopped when they caught a glimpse of a new story about a murder that happened locally.

What was thought to be just an electrical fire at the residence of a Nanticoke man is found to be arson. After crews extinguished the two-story residence, firefighters discovered Dustin Kandrac, the manager of a local Kentucky Fried Chicken, shot through the chest. A note was found stuffed in the mouth of the victim which reads "Tag, You're It!" The whole community is in shock over the murder that happened this afternoon in the once quiet city of Nanticoke. Law enforcement is asking for help by asking local residences or businesses to turn in any surveillance video around the location of this home.

"Bonnie?"

"Yeah," Bonnie replied, still staring at the news of the day.

"Take a look at their mouths, Bonnie."

"I can't see their mouth, Donna. They have respirators on."

"No... look. Their respirator masks. Look, at John. Right now. The mask is moving. And now it stopped. Now, look at Yüsli. His is moving. Now it's back to John. Um, Bonnie, I think they may be talking to each other."

"What? No, that's impossible." Bonnie watched closely. Every single time John's mask stopped moving, Yüsli's started to move.

*****

"The EKG shows no unusual activity," Dr. Grant said, making sure his equipment was functioning correctly for the third time. "I seriously doubt they are talking to each other."

"They have to be! Look at their masks!"

Dr. Grant didn't. He stared at Bonnie.

"I said look at them!"

Ed looked at them once again to please Bonnie. It certainly did look like they were talking to each other, but it just wasn't possible.

"I don't know what to say, ladies. This equipment would show any brain activity." He disconnected the machine again and apologized for what seemed like the 20th time since they arrived at the hospital. "I'm sorry, I have patients I need to attend."

Just as he was about to leave, he heard a thud and a scream. The thud came from Bonnie crashing to the floor, and the scream came from Donna.

CHAPTER FIFTEEN

"Yüsli, listen. A third Darth Vader. What the hell? Hello? Who's there?"

"Oh my God, hun, is that you?"

"Bonnie!"

The only thing Yüsli heard for the next few seconds was sobbing. *Get over it, you guys!*

"Hun, what's going on? Where am I? How did I get here? Am I going to fall through these clouds?"

"Yüsli and I have no idea what's going on. We don't know how we got here either. What about you? How did you get here? And no, you're not going to fall. It takes some time to get used to, but take baby steps. You'll see."

"But there's no floor. It's just mist."

"I know. Trust your husband. Walk."

Bonnie took baby steps, and to her amazement, she didn't fall through the clouds. She finally answered John's question. "I don't know how I got here. The last thing I remember was sitting in the hospital with you two."

"The hospital? What? You mean we're not dead?" said Yüsli, relieved and now even more scared. "How did we get there?"

"Probably the same way I got here. I can't remember anything from a few minutes ago. How far back can you remember?"

"I don't know how much time is missing from my memory, hun, but Yüsli and I have been working hard to figure things out. We think we're in Yüsli's dream, well, the end of it anyway. He found a bucket of chicken."

Bonnie didn't know if this was bizarro world or what the heck John was talking about. "Bucket of chicken…"

"Yeah, remember you saw Yüsli's dream? Colonel Sanders held a gun to someone's head and made him drive to KFC?"

"Um… yeah?"

"Well, Yüsli found a bucket of chicken."

"Oh… kay…"

Bonnie knew she would have some type of brain damage like she thought her husband did.

"It's true, Bonnie," Yüsli confirmed, "And the reason there's nothing all around us is that my dream ended."

"But that was days ago. What about my dream, you know, the one with the clown? Why am I in Yüsli's dream and not mine?"

"Are you thinking what I'm thinking, Yüsli?"

"Yup! Probably."

"Hun, feel around with your feet. Swish the mist around, slowly, with long strides. Tell me if you kick something."

Yes, my husband's brain is dying. I'm already considering myself dead.

"What are you talking about?"

John made a slight mistake. This has to be information overload for her. "I'm sorry, hun, we'll try that later. Just take it easy, let me know when you're more comfortable with things."

"I'll never be comfortable here. I'm not leaving this spot. Why haven't you come to me? Don't you miss me?"

John realized he was feeding her too much information at once. "You wouldn't believe how much I missed you." John took quite some time to explain things, as much as he knew, very slowly and calmly. With the dozens of questions he couldn't answer, Bonnie at least knew what John knew.

While John was explaining everything, Bonnie got more comfortable walking. "So, what's this swishing of the foot thing?"

"Well, I found a gun by swishing, just like I explained. Then Yüsli found that bucket of chicken. So if you swish, let's see what you find. I'm sure there will be something. Or, at least, I hope so."

Bonnie must have been an expert swisher because, on her first try, her foot hit something.

"You mean like that?" Bonnie laughed.

"Wait, you found something already? What is it?"

"I don't know yet. It rolled away."

She got down on her hands and knees and felt around. She moved too quickly causing the rubber object to roll away once again. "It's rubber, whatever it is, but it rolled away again."

"Be careful," Yüsli said, more anxious than both of them to find out what it could be.

"Here it is."

Bonnie grabbed hold of it and brought it out from the mist.

"Um… It looks like a rubber nose."

Yüsli started to laugh. "Ok, so a gun, a bucket of chicken, and a rubber nose. We're getting somewhere, guys, I think, aren't we?"

"It makes sense, though. Didn't that clown in your dream have a rubber nose?"

"Yes, it most certainly did. I know this is the one from my dream because of the splotchy red glitter pattern on it. I remember it well! Are we all in my dream now?"

"I think we're supposed to use these items somehow to solve a puzzle and get out of here," John said. "I'm wondering if we have to get everybody here who wore The Andervoge and use all of their items to escape."

"I hope not. That would be a lot of people, Yüsli. One of them is back in Singapore, so that wouldn't work anyway."

"Oh no."

"Don't worry, hun, I'm sure that's not what we're supposed to do."

Only a few hours into it, Bonnie was stressed and started to cry.

"I'm sorry, please don't cry. We'll get out of this. Let's put our heads together and think. So the last thing you remember is being in the hospital. Are we all in a coma?"

"The doctor said it isn't a coma, but I think it is. It has to be. He's never seen this type of condition before. Donna was with us in the room, and I have a feeling she's going to be here soon, too. I was the third person to wear this stupid thing, and now I'm the third person here. She was next. I told you not to go ahead with this stupid thing."

CHAPTER SIXTEEN

There they slept, or whatever condition they were in, all three of them, side by side. Donna was wearing out the carpet by pacing back and forth, wondering when it would be her time. Dr. Grant felt horrible for leaving her alone, but there was nothing else he could do, plus he was backed up with patients that needed attention.

She hung up the phone after speaking with her aunt, Angie Litchkowski, and was somewhat happy to hear that she was able to book an immediate flight from Florida and would be on her way soon. Donna knew that Angie couldn't help the situation in any way, but was comforted in knowing that someone cared enough to fly out in a moments notice and take care of her son for *when* something DOES happens.

Donna was too afraid to leave the hospital. *When* this happens to her, and she knew it would, at least she would already be in the hospital and be taken care of instead of driving home, blanking out, and having an accident. She called off work once again, and relaxed in a chair alongside all three of them, wondering how to warn the others who wore this of their pending doom. There would be no sleep tonight for her, that she also knew.

Hours passed, as Donna sat in the very uncomfortable chair watching reruns of *Who's The Boss*, thinking that maybe a comedy would cheer her up. It didn't. Donna was dead-tired but couldn't fall asleep because she was afraid that when/if she woke up, she would be in the same state they were in. It was seven hours later when another breaking news report flashed across the screen.

"We now have the very first photograph of the individual who may be involved in the *Tag, You're It* killings. A few hours ago, a second victim was found with the same handwritten note, *Tag, You're it,* stuffed in his mouth. 27-year-old Nemanja Stanic, a traveling clown at our yearly circus event, was found in his apartment with a bullet through his chest, same precise location of impact as the previous victim. The bullet is also identical to the one that killed Dustin Kandrac, a local Kentucky Fried Chicken manager. The gunshot was heard around 4:35 p.m. by a local resident. It is still unknown if this is a serial or copycat killer. This image was captured from a local resident's surveillance video. If anyone knows who this man is or his whereabouts, please dial 911 immediately. Do not confront this individual. He is considered armed and dangerous."

Wait a minute. That man. He looks familiar. Donna couldn't place the face of where she saw this person before. And then it hit her all at once - like a freight train.

*****

"Okay, we have to figure this out."

Dr. Grant checked his flipchart. "Well, we know John has been here for a full week, which is around the same time this lunatic killed his first victim. Are you sure this is the same guy?"

"Yes. I'd go home to get the video to prove it, but I can't take the risk of me passing out during the drive home."

"No, that's OK, I understand," Dr. Grant said, scratching his chin. "So you had a dream of the killer before he killed? This doesn't make any sense. I can't see how any of this is possible. Is that dream machine telling the future or something?"

Donna didn't answer. Dr. Grant wasn't expecting one.

"That news clip said the incident happened at 4:35. That's the same time Bonnie collapsed to the floor. Coincidence? I think not." She looked back over at the trio and pointed. "Look, they can't be in a coma. They're all talking to each other!"

94

Ed looked over at all three of them. Sure enough, once one mouth stopped moving, the next one started to move. Sometimes two did at once, but he assumed they were talking over each other.

"Now what?"

"I have a dumb idea. I got no sleep last night because of everything running through my mind, so I had a lot of time to think. All I could come up with is, maybe, if we put The Andervoge on one of them, it will record something, that is, if their minds are active. I know they are doing something, I see their legs keep moving too like they are walking. I know they have to be interacting."

"Do you know how to operate it?"

Donna thought about it for a moment, and her eyes lit up with excitement. "Yes, actually, I do! John told me the secret method of starting it up!"

"Well, if you want to do it, by all means, go for it. All you have to do is get a hold of the thing. I don't want any part of putting that on any one of them."

"Here's my number. If I'm not back in thirty minutes, will you promise to have someone look for me?"

Ed nodded a firm yes. "Please, be careful. If I were you, I'd call for a taxi or an Uber, something…"

"Yeah, that's what I'm going to do. There's no

way I'm driving. I need to get out of here anyway, I'm going crazy."

*****

Lucky for Donna, the back garage door to Bonnie's home was unlocked. She felt guilty about going through their house, but there it was, right where Bonnie said John's last customer left it – on her bed. She flipped the joystick in the secret method explained to her last month. When the lights lit up the way they did previously, she was relieved that the secret code wasn't changed.

CHAPTER SEVENTEEN

"I don't want any part of what you're about to do. You do it. You're going to have to put it on someone."

Donna couldn't be angry. Dr. Grant was right. No one knew what this thing did to them or what it could do if they wore it while in the state that they are in.

"Fine." As horrible as the thought was, she picked the person she knew the least, which happened to be Yüsli. Dr. Grant didn't want to be a part of it, but he sure had an interest as to what she was doing.

The Andervoge was placed on Yüsli's head. She glanced over at the doctor, who was obviously trying to hide his impatience as to what was about to unfold. She focused back on Yüsli, moved the joystick, and the device lit up. Immediately, the light starting to flash which was an indication it was recording. The timer started its count. The new tiny monitor showed a misty fog. She turned back to face the doctor bearing a huge smile. "The movie is about to start."

"Cancel the rest of my appointments today," the Doctor called out to the head receptionist."

*****

Donna and Dr. Grant listened to the conversation taking place from the sound coming through the miniature speaker, still waiting for a picture to emerge.

"John, you got us into this mess, you have to get us out."

"Hun, don't you think if I knew how Yüsli and I would be out by now? I don't know where this mess is. I don't know how we got here. My question is, why didn't you do something earlier when I called you before, you could have called for help then."

"What? Called me? When?"

"What do you mean when? I called you in a panic, saying there's just mist around me. You asked me to take a picture, but I was unable to send it because my battery was too low."

"Did he say just mist around me? Um, is this what they're seeing," Dr. Grant said, waiting for something else to come into focus.

"I don't know. This screen wasn't here when I had it on my head. Maybe it takes some time for the picture to come into focus. Ssshh, let's listen to what they're talking about. It's very hard to hear with such a small speaker."

"John, you never called me. Look at my call history. Oh crap, my battery is nearly flat!"

"Damn! Does this place drain your battery or something? Hurry, call someone!"

"And who do you expect me to call and just what do I tell them? Never mind, too late. It just switched off. It's dead."

"Don't say that word. Yüsli, what about your phone?"

"I don't have it. I guess I wasn't carrying one when I arrived."

*****

"Hello? Can anyone hear me," Donna said directly into The Andervoge's video screen, feeling like an idiot. Sure enough, there was a response.

"Donna? Is that you? I can barely hear you", John said. "Are you here with us?"

Dr. Grant gave Donna a high-five.

"Yeah, it's me, Donna. I'm not where you are. What I do know is…"

*****

No one could hear Donna clearly except Yüsli since he was the one wearing The Andervoge. After they realized this, it was soon moved to John since it was his invention. Donna and Ed were able to inform them they're not dead, that they are alive in a hospital bed, and most importantly, the psycho from her dreams is the one killing.

John told her all he knew, too. That there's nothing in this dream world, that they don't need to sleep or eat, and how it's the most boring thing in the world. He immediately knew who Donna was referring to when she mentioned the killer, and told her that this guy was also in every single dream he recorded.

"And you let me think it was a real dream? When you get out of there, I want a refund," Donna said, trying to lighten up the situation.

John was now sure that the photo he took when he first arrived had to be creepy Billy. He also explained the mysterious objects which appeared in each person's dream.

"Wait a minute. A clown nose, and a bucket of chicken?"

"Yeah, why," John asked. "Do you know how these are connected?"

Dr. Grant spoke up because now all of a sudden he wanted to get involved. He leaned down to John's ear. "This doesn't make much sense, John, but the first person this guy killed was a manager at KFC. KFC, chicken? And then his next victim was a clown at a circus. Clown, nose?"

"Ok, finally something that makes sense, I think." John let them know about the connection of the objects in Yüsli and Bonnie's dreams. "These are the only items we found, other than the gun I used, and we're the only ones stuck here, that I know of anyway," John exclaimed with hopes that they may be getting somewhere. "I'm assuming someone else died if we find another object, but at least I'll know who it is by what we find."

"If Sponge Bob winds up dead, my kid isn't going to be happy." Donna was trying to once again lighten up the situation because she knew she was next in line to fall into this dream-like state, with someone else possibly dying because of her. It was just a matter of time. Oh, how she wished her aunt would get here already to take care of her son instead of the babysitter who's there with him now.

After the continued discussion, John's only suggestion was for her to call all of his previous customers to see how they're doing. She was asked to personally make these calls, pretending to be John's new secretary doing a follow-up and was given a strict instruction not to mention the state he's in so it won't cause any panic.

Donna hired another Uber. Her first stop was at her house to grab the DVD of her dream so she can show the doctor. Next, was Bonnie's house, to search the huge stack of messy paperwork of customer records and make some calls. John knew it would be a while and had time to think about what could have gone wrong with his invention.

"Everything was fine until I went to live mode, Bonnie. That has to be it. I recorded quite a few dreams without problems and hundreds, maybe even thousands, of my dreams. The first time I use live mode, this happens? I'm sure that the creepy guy was willing me to do this. Maybe he even gave me the idea somehow through telepathy. He wanted to get out, and the live mode made it happen. And since it *was* live, he was able to escape. Now he's hopping from dream to dream of the people who used it."

"Whatever it is, hun, I'm sorry, your business is over. I will not have any part of this in our home any longer, and I will not place anyone else in danger."

John knew it was over anyway, although he was trying to hold onto the micro-slim chance that none of this was his fault. Ten years of his life down the drain. Even though technically he was responsible for the murders, he had no plans of destroying the device and wanted to hold on to it until he can come up with a solution.

"I know, hun. I know."

CHAPTER EIGHTEEN

The guilt finally got to John. He couldn't lie any longer, not to himself, not to his fiancé, not to anyone. Maybe it would help to admit it, out loud, what he knew right from the beginning, would help ease his pain.

"Hun, um, guys, I have a confession to make. I don't know how to say this, and I should have mentioned it from the start. I have had a very long time to think about this since I never sleep, so please, don't interrupt me."

"You know where we are, don't you? We're stuck here forever, aren't we?"

"No, no, it's nothing like that. I don't know what is happening right now but listen to me. All of those customer dreams weren't dreams."

Bonnie hesitated, wondering if she should speak. She did when there was silence for a few seconds. "I think we all know that already, hun. At least I did. That's what I told you from the beginning, and you denied it. If they weren't dreams, what were they?"

"The moment you suggested it, I knew you were right, but I didn't want to give up hope. I don't know what these images are. I'm sorry, but I'm not done speaking. What I want to confess is this guy was in every single customer dream I ever recorded. Every single one, hun."

"I kind of figured that, too. I purposely didn't want to see any more after I realized it wasn't working properly. Why did you continue to use it?"

"The only reason I continued is to see where this would go. People were paying, and I was greedy. I thought I'd eventually figure out why he was in every dream if I kept going, but I honestly didn't know it would come to this. Now since two people are dead, maybe more we don't know about yet, I can't hold back the guilt any longer. If we ever get out of here, I will destroy that thing, I promise," John lied.

"You should have told me."

It's a good thing the only thing John could see is the mist surrounding him and not the expression on Bonnie's face.

"And if I did tell you, then what? Would you have suggested not using it anymore? No, you would have simply done what I was doing. Kept using it to see what would happen next and let the easy money keep coming in. Am I right?"

"No, I…"

John interrupted rudely, now his guilt turning to anger at himself. "Yes, Bonnie, you wouldn't say stop using it. There was no reason to stop. The few times I've used it on actual customers, we made easy money. It was very interesting to see what would happen in the next dream. Since my customers had no idea what was in my other customer's dreams, they honestly thought that's what they were dreaming. Or maybe this device forced those images in their mind, and it created their dream for them."

"If you'd have let me finish, you would know that I was going to say no, I wouldn't stop you from using it, but I would have questioned the validity of the dreams."

"Sorry."

"So now what do we do?"

"I don't know," John sighed, "Take it one step at a time. We'll see what Donna finds out about the other customers. I have no idea of what the connection is going to be between the person who wore it and the victim this freak kills, other than the death relates to someone in the dream, like where they work, so there's no way to predict anything. Since Donna is the next one I used this on and she had a dream about Sponge Bob, I don't see how anyone could die unless they live in a pineapple under the sea. If she doesn't end up here with us, I'll know that I need to get rid of that live feature when we get out of this place. She was the next person I used this on."

"No, it's not safe, and it's not their dreams. You said it yourself. That thing must be destroyed as soon as we get out of here. You promised me, John."

John didn't say a word. He knew it would have to be destroyed but would hate to see ten years of his life go down the toilet.

"You're right," John finally said, but Bonnie knew he wouldn't do it. She'd have to destroy it behind his back.

*****

"Donna said almost all people are accounted for," John shouted to everyone in the mist world. They weren't able to hear the conversation except for his responses to what Donna was telling him through The Andervoge.

"Donna couldn't get a hold of everyone," John continued to yell. "No one else killed…. Still not caught…. No clues as to where he is…."

"You don't have to shout, John, we can hear you just fine. Just fill us in at the end of your conversation," Bonnie snapped back. She was getting agitated, being bored to death for so long.

Between every single patient Dr. Grant had, he came to check on Donna's progress. Each time it was only for a minute or so, and that's all he could spare.

"Hey, are you ok," he said as he walked past the open door. Donna's eyes went up into her eyelids. She fell off the bed, crashing into the hospital cart, spilling water and the tray of food all over the floor. This room was about to get very crowded.

*****

As much as Dr. Grant wanted to call in an assistant to temporarily take over his position, he knew it would be senseless since there's nothing he can do for them. He wasn't about to stay and have a chat with everyone in dreamland. He'd only need to keep everyone informed of what's going on when he had bad news to share. By the sounds of their

106

conversation, everyone was already welcoming
Donna to dreamland.

CHAPTER NINTEEN

"There it is, guys." Donna swished her foot once more hitting an object. She already knew about how things operate there in dreamland, knowing she can't fall through the mist and the finding of the objects.

"See? Told you it would work. What is it? Wait. Don't tell me," John laughed, "your dream had Sponge Bob in it. So – it's a sponge."

"Glad you find this funny," Bonnie said, sick to her stomach that her husband was enjoying this when someone else was probably dead.

"Hun, look, there's nothing we can do about this. No, it's not funny, but I'm certainly not going to sulk about it either. There's nothing we can do. Be happy we're not all dead."

Hating to hear the bickering, Donna interrupted. "You're wrong, John. It's a hot dog."

This time, Yüsli laughed. It seemed like Bonnie was the only one who wasn't amused.

"No," John corrected, "It's a Krusty Dog," remembering that's what Sponge Bob invented in Donna's dream. "Please don't eat it like Yüsli did with the chicken that he found."

"Hey, that stuff was damn good. Go ahead, Donna, I dare you. Tell us what a Krusty Dog tastes like since they don't exist."

"I'm not eating this," Donna chuckled. Yes, even she seemed to be enjoying this.

"We can't keep screwing around like this, guys. We have to figure out how the hell to get out of this place before more people die!" Bonnie was now infuriated.

"Hey doc, are you there?"

There wasn't a response, so John assumed he was tending to patients.

"I hope he called my Aunt," Donna said, extremely worried about her son but trying not to get too depressed. Luckily he was too young to realize what was going on, but she had faith in getting out of this place, and her son was her inspiration to try harder. She also knew if they all put their minds together, they'd be out in no time.

"Hey, John, here's a thought. I wonder what would happen if the live view feature was removed and another dream was recorded. If this creep got out into the real world, that means he shouldn't be in any new dreams, right? So if the live view is gone, would that destroy him?

And what would the dream look like without this guy in it? Would your invention work properly?"

"No," Bonnie said immediately, hoping to stop any hair-brained ideas John was about to get. Oh, how she wished Donna never suggested that idea. "That's a horrible idea. That creep was in dreams before the live mode. And anyway, when someone gets their dream recorded, someone else dies."

"Not necessarily true, hun." John's passion immediately kicked in. He quickly came up with an excuse, convinced by his inner greed that it was a good idea. "I think Donna may have something here. If this creep is already out there, will the use of this on someone else force him to come back? Maybe that's the way out! Having him come back, and we'll all be free!"

"Who are you trying to bullshit? That makes no sense. He won't be able to get back here if live mode is removed. And if by some miracle that he does, we'll probably be stuck here with him, too! You said you got a picture of him before the live view was added! And anyway, who's going to be stupid enough to get their dream recorded now?"

"No one knows I'm here, right? No one knows the connection between the murders and the dreams, and nothing of what's happening here in mist world is on the news, right? My voicemail probably has a thousand messages wanting to book an appointment. We can choose one of those, as long as someone can access my phone from the real world."

110

"Oh, what a shame. We don't have anyone that can help use The Andervoge."

"I'll do it," Dr. Grant said immediately through The Andervoge to mist world, without hesitation and apparently before he changed his mind. "I'm watching the news. We need to do something, right now. There has been another death, guys. This man has to be stopped."

"The Tag, You're It" serial killer has struck again, this time in New York City. Marie Nagy, Age 44, a jewelry street vendor, was shot in broad daylight. The bullet struck the precise location to the millimeter as the other two previous victims. It's unclear how the suspect escaped. Video footage from many local businesses shows this man just "disappearing" into mid-air after turning a corner. He's believed to be not only an expert marksman but also an illusionist. The same type of hand-written note was found in the mouth of the victim. Law enforcement warns everyone to be on high alert as it appears this man is moving from city to city and state to state. So far there are no leads, motive or a connection between any of the victims.

CHAPTER TWENTY

John certainly made the live mode feature easy to remove. A simple micro-usb removal and tug on the monitor made it pop right off.

You have twenty-seven new messages. Dr. Grant had his computer on, ready to go, with a new spreadsheet opened. Headers were programmed and color-coded with date called, time called, caller name and notes. He sat there with John's phone, going through the full voice mailbox, not deleting any messages just so no new ones would be able to be added. It took him nearly an hour to go through and log all the calls. About twenty-five percent were repeated callers asking if he got his previous voicemail, and then some extremely irate and irrational callers having the audacity that they demand a return call. *Sigh.*

Ed was instructed to choose anyone he wanted, and Ed's choice was Joe Domkowski, the kindest, sweetest man from all the twenty-seven voicemails. Even the third voicemail that Joe left was overly polite. Ed placed the call, entering all numbers and hesitating before hitting send, wondering if he made the right decision. *Will someone else die?* He closed his eyes and hit send.

"Hello," the soothing voice said.

"Hi, Joe," said Ed, not even asking if this was Joe or not. Joe's voice was super soft and comfortable. "This is Dr. Ed Grant. I'm calling

113

you about setting up an appointment with The Andervoge."

"Oh, thank you for calling me back, sir. I was wondering if everything was ok. I was beginning to get concerned."

Yeah, this man is a sweetheart. "Yes, I'm ok," Ed said, failing to mention he's not the inventor of the device. The less he has to explain the better, even though the guilt already hit him. "When would you like to come in?"

"Whenever you want, sir. Whatever is *most* convenient for you."

"I apologize it took so long for me to return your call. We've been swamped. An opening just came in tonight, if that's ok with you." Ed hoped he sounded just as kind-hearted as Joe did to him.

"Yes, that is fine, sir. I usually go to bed around seven o'clock," said Joe, "and I'm usually up around four a.m."

Ed realized Joe must be a sweet little old man. *Who else goes to bed at seven o'clock. And old people usually wake up at wee hours in the morning.* "Do you have transportation?"

"Yes, sir, I do. I can be there at five o'clock if you want to grab a cup of coffee with me. We can have a good ol' chat."

Yes, Joe is definitely the sweetest old man he's ever heard. Probably a lonely old man as well, from the sound of it. Ed didn't plan on spending a lot of time on this, he just wanted to get this over with but how can he say no?

"Sure. Five o'clock sounds great." Ed gave him the address of The Lounge, and twenty minutes later, after trying to get him off the phone discussing everything under the sun, they hung up. *Sigh.*

He instructed his receptionist to once again cancel the rest of his appointments for the rest of the night through tomorrow afternoon. Ed ignored the irritated look on the receptionist's face. This was way too important.

*****

"You're joking, right?" Ed couldn't stop laughing at Joe's stories.

Ed knew Joe would arrive well before five, so he was well prepared. But now at 7:45, with several cups of coffee in their system, Ed was now afraid Joe would now never get to sleep. Joe noticed Ed kept looking at his watch.

"Oh, I'm sorry, sir. I must be keeping you from your daily activities. Let's get this dream thing started so you can get on with your business."

"It's no problem, Joe, I'm having a great time, but yeah, you're right, let's get started."

Ed got The Andervoge placed on Joe and activated it with the instructions given to him earlier. When the lights didn't come on as expected, Ed looked a little nervous."

"Everything alright, sir?" Joe may be elderly, but he's certainly observant.

Ed tried again, realizing the step he missed. "Yeah, here we go. Remember, call me when you're ready. I'll hear you through the cameras."

The lounge door was closed, and by the time Ed got to John's desk, Joe was already out cold, even with all that coffee in his system.

Visit www.bryankollar.com/joe.html
to view Joe's dream

Ed was disappointed that Billy was still in this dream, not out of dream world, and realized two things. First, that Billy was Santiago's first name. And second, if another murder occurred, technically he'd be the one responsible for it. He also now knew that John's invention didn't work but dreaded the thought of telling him.

The whole dream was about a group of people having a meeting about how they are going to kill Santiago, the name he heard mentioned several times before. There were about thirty people in this dream. They all headed to Santiago's house, entered his bedroom and killed him in cold blood like he's been doing in the real world. Dr. Grant got excited thinking this meant Santiago was dead. But at the end of the dream, another Santiago bursts through the door kills everyone with a bomb, blowing up his own house and everyone in it, including himself.

He had a sickening feeling in his stomach this dream was trying to tell him if Santiago was killed, he would only come back to kill some more.

116

It's only a matter of time before someone turns up dead. What have I done?

*****

"I'm sorry," Dr. Grant spoke into John's ear. "Billy Santiago was still in Joe's dream." Ed felt he didn't have to mention that John's invention doesn't work. John already knew.

"Billy Santiago? So that's how those names are connected. We now have a full name. Maybe somehow this can be reported anonymously to the police? Well, I think it was worth doing since we have this new information. Thanks for helping. We may need your help again, though, if that's ok," John said. "We were throwing some ideas around and would like to discuss them with you."

"I'm sorry, I don't want to put that on someone again. I will consider reporting this name anonymously, but I know I'm already going to be responsible for another death at some point."

"No, no, Ed, it's nothing like that. We were wondering what would happen if one of us were off our respirator. I mean, when Bonnie found Yüsli, he was passed out cold and coughing until the ambulance arrived and put him on the respirator."

There was no response.

"Hello?"

"I'm here. I'm just thinking about this suggestion. Why would you want to go into a coughing fit?"

"Well, wait… Now, when Bonnie passed out, you said you witnessed the same thing. Her breathing was irregular, that's why she was put on one too. But what if the respirator was left off for an extended period of time?"

"I don't understand why you'd want to try this. Again, it's obvious you'd go into a coughing fit again," Ed said.

"And die," Bonnie said, still hesitant about anything her husband wanted to do. She was even angrier that someone else was going to die.

"As I said, Bonnie, that's exactly my point. If Yüsli died – in here, wherever 'here' is, would he come back to life, there?"

After another lengthy pause, Ed finally spoke up. "That's an interesting idea. I assume Yüsli is volunteering?"

"Yup. I'm dead already. I would've killed myself by now, but I can't. There isn't anything to do it with! It's my life. Do it, now. Pull the plug. I have completely lost my mind in this God forsaken place."

"I don't want to be responsible for killing anyone else. Again, I already know there's going to be another death because of Joe's dream."

"No, I want you to do this. Right now. Pull the damn plug. No matter what happens. No matter how much I choke. Leave the damn plug out. Do it."

Even though The Andervoge wasn't on Yüsli's head, he was heard with a booming voice, probably because he screamed it at the top of his lungs.

After ten seconds of silence, the booming spoke again. "I said do it! NOW!"

At that moment, Dr. Grant pulled the plug. Within a few seconds, Yüsli went into a coughing fit. His breathing became erratic. Ed held the plug in his hand, ready for the worst. A full ten seconds of Yüsli's choking worsening, Ed leaned over, ready to plug it back in.

"I said do it, damn you, coward!"

What the heck?

"Um, Yüsli, I did. You're off the respirator."

"Knock it off, stop being a douche, and pull the plug," the non-coughing and perfectly normal dream-land Yüsli said while the other Yüsli in the real world continued to breathe erratically.

"Yüsli, I'm serious. You're off the respirator. You breathing here is horrible."

"Well, I feel fine, here. Are you sure the plug is out?"

"What do you mean am I sure? I'm holding the plug in my hand right now," Grant said.

"So much for that idea."

"Well, wait, let's see what happens here if he stays off this thing."

Every minute that respirator was unplugged, Yüsli worsened. And every minute it was unplugged, Dr. Grant kept asking Yüsli *are you ok* until he was told to shut the hell up and not speak another word. Even though he wasn't happy with Yüsli right now, he had no choice but to sit there and wait for the inevitable. After fifteen minutes, the coughing stopped and he heard a "Hello?" The voice was heard loud and clear, not from the tiny speaker.

Yüsli's eyes fluttered open.

"Oh my God, I can see you!"

CHAPTER TWENTY ONE

Yüsli bolted upright. "I'm back! Oh my God, I'm back!!"

"John, is Yüsli still there in dream world, too?"

"Yüsli? Yüsli???"

No response from the land of the mist.

"No, he's not! Did he survive? Is he there?"

Yüsli talked directly into The Andervoge even though he felt really stupid doing so. "Yes. John, it worked! I'm back, baby!!"

John hadn't felt this excited since he completed his invention. "Bonnie, my love, what do ya say, want to get the heck out of here?"

"Hell, yeah," said Bonnie, now extremely confident in her husband.

Dr. Grant already had his hand on Bonnie's respirator power cord. Yüsli had one hand on Donna's power cord, and the other on John's.

"Well, what are you waiting for?"

All three power cords were pulled at the same time.

*****

"Come on, John, I know you could do it."

All four of them – Donna, Ed, Yüsli, and Bonnie stood alongside John's hospital bed. John struggled to breathe and was even worse than what happened with Yüsli.

It was so bad that Dr. Grant desperately wanted to plug it back in, but John insisted he was doing just fine.

"Guys, listen to me. Do I sound like I'm in pain? I'm not. I'm not having any difficulty even in the slightest. I don't care what my body is doing out there. It's not affecting me here, so do not plug that back in no matter how long it takes or how bad it seems like it's getting! Promise me!"

"I can't promise, hun. What if it's causing damage to your body here? What if your lungs can't take it and when you do get out of there, you really won't be able to breathe?"

"Look, I don't have a choice. I'm not staying here. It's a risk I'm going to have to take. Now leave it unplugged, please."

The cardiac monitor flatlined.

"Um, John, you just flatlined."

No response.

"John??"

Still no response. Ed grabbed the power cord.

"John!"

"Just kidding. I'm here. I don't care if I flatlined. As I stated before, do not plug that in no matter what happens out there. I'm fine."

"You idiot, John, you almost gave me a heart attack."

Not proud of his joke, John frowned and felt guilty. "Sorry."

"Well, now you've just stopped coughing too. Are you sure?"

"No response."

"Knock it off, John, it worked the first time, it's not going to work again."

John opened his eyes and looked at every one of them, staring down at him.

"I'm back."

After everyone hugged each other for nearly a half hour, they all parted ways. Yüsli went home to his empty house. The first thing he did was pick up his cell phone from the kitchen table and grab a beer from the fridge. *I guess that's why I didn't have it in the dream world. It wasn't in my pocket.* He checked his voice mail. Four new voicemails. The first one was from his boss, asking if he was coming into work. The second message was from his angry boss, telling him to get to work right now. The third message was from is irate boss telling him if he doesn't show up for work today, don't bother coming in tomorrow. The final message was from his very pissed off boss yelling two simple words. *You're Fired.*

"Jerk," Yüsli said to no one but himself. There was no way he could call his boss now and explain what happened, simply because he couldn't explain it himself. His job of 12 years – gone. There's no way he would be able to find another aircraft maintenance technician job, and at age 50, who would hire him for what he was making?

Bonnie's voicemail was very different. She had a tad more from her boss and co-workers, but instead of her boss saying *you're fired*, each voicemail showed concern. *We're worried about you, Bon, call me* type of messages.

And John? He worked from home, so the only thing he had to deal with is the twenty-seven voicemails, a full voice mailbox from people who wanted to have their dreams recorded, and the 225 orders he was backed up on packing up over the past two weeks. Negative feedback was left by quite a few angry customers who didn't get their precious coffee order in the promised three-day arrival guarantee.

Bonnie rubbed his shoulders as John placed the tiny LCD screen back in place and connected the USB cable. He then held the contraption in his hand, turning it over and over again. She felt bad for him. *He did put a lot of work into that project.*

"Look, hun, I know this is hard to do. We have to destroy that thing."

"But why? Seriously. We're all safe. No one is in dream world."

"Because Santiago may still be out there, and maybe the only way for him to die is to destroy this thing. He's probably trapped in the real world."

"We've been out of there for a full week now. We would've known about another killing if he was still doing it. Either way, there's no way to know if he's going to go away by destroying it, so why get rid of ten years of work? How about this? If we hear about another killing, then I'll destroy it. Fair enough?"

"No, John. It's the right thing to do. You know it, John, you don't want to admit it. And again, you said it yourself, they are not dreams, and I hate to remind you, this invention didn't work from the start."

John knew his fiancé was right. It had to be destroyed.

"I can't. I'm sorry. If you think this needs to be destroyed, you're going to have to do it." He handed The Andervoge over to his wife and left the room, ready to burst into tears. Bonnie held it in her hands for a few seconds. She left the room and got in her car, placing it gently on the seat next to her. John saw it all from the bedroom window on the upper floor. *Where's she going? To destroy and bury it somewhere?*

Bonnie drove for only five minutes, only enough to make sure he couldn't see which way she went. She drove far enough where she knew she couldn't be seen anymore, got out of her car, opened the passenger door, and grabbed The Andervoge. She then popped the trunk. The tire iron was lifted from its holster and pushed to the side to get access to the blanket way in the back.

The old ratty blanket was the perfect size to cover The Andervoge.

She stood there for what seemed like minutes, staring into the sky. The Andervoge was pushed all back, far in the corner of the trunk. Since she was the only one who ever drove this car, John would never know his device is still safe and sound. She didn't have the heart to destroy it either. When the trunk was closed, she wasn't able to see the glow coming from the screen or hear the tiny voice coming from the speaker say "Hello? Is anyone there?"

Bio

When I'm not writing books, I repair computer equipment throughout the Northeast PA area.

I also own my own coffee business! If you have a Keurig, you'll love all the flavors I offer (over 120!) Check out www.BryanKollar.com